*Brave Sydney-based medics, putting their lives—
and hearts—on the line!*

Led by maverick ER consultant Blake Cooper,
Bondi Bayside Hospital's Specialist Disaster Response
team is ready for action!

Handpicked for being among the best in their fields,
these courageous men and women are trained to be
first responders, rescuing and treating survivors of
crisis situations, and they'll risk everything to save
lives. But when the pressure is on and danger is all
around, the biggest risk of all is falling in love!

The Shy Nurse's Rebel Doc by Alison Roberts
Finding His Wife, Finding a Son by Marion Lennox

Available now!

Healed by Her Army Doc by Meredith Webber
Rescued by Her Mr. Right by Alison Roberts

Available next month!

Dear Reader,

As I get older and hopefully wiser, I realize that the most precious gift in life is friendship. It's a concept that's a bit diluted these days thanks to social media, but we all know what true friendship is— that family you get to choose for yourself.

Sharing things with those true friends cements those bonds and creates the memories that shine when you look back. When those friends are fellow authors and you can share creating something together, it's really special.

This Bondi Bay Heroes series is a collaboration with Marion Lennox and Meredith Webber and I've been lucky enough to "bookend" it with the first and last stories.

I'd like to welcome you into the world of this specialist disaster relief team and into the hearts of the people involved.

Let's start with Blake. And Sam…

Happy reading!

With love,

Alison xx

THE SHY NURSE'S
REBEL DOC

———

ALISON ROBERTS

HARLEQUIN® MEDICAL ROMANCE™

Recycling programs
for this product may
not exist in your area.

ISBN-13: 978-1-335-66364-1

The Shy Nurse's Rebel Doc

First North American Publication 2018

Copyright © 2018 by Alison Roberts

Printed in U.S.A.

Books by Alison Roberts

Harlequin Medical Romance

Rescued Hearts

The Doctor's Wife for Keeps
Twin Surprise for the Italian Doc

Christmas in Manhattan

Sleigh Ride with the Single Dad

Paddington Children's Hospital

A Life-Saving Reunion

Christmas Eve Magic

Their First Family Christmas

Wildfire Island Docs

The Nurse Who Stole His Heart
The Fling That Changed Everything

The Surrogate's Unexpected Miracle

Harlequin Romance

The Baby Who Saved Christmas
The Forbidden Prince

Visit the Author Profile page
at Harlequin.com for more titles.

For Linda and Meredith, with much love.

CHAPTER ONE

IT BLINDSIDED HIM.

Blake Cooper had just swung himself off his motorbike in his allotted ED staff parking space at Sydney's Bondi Bayside Hospital and flipped up his visor. He should have been easing off his helmet, now, and reaching for the worn leather satchel in the side pannier but he wasn't moving at all. His fingers felt like they were stuck to the sides of his helmet and his eyes were just as stuck.

On that car…

A gleaming, vintage MG roadster.

Red.

Of course it was red. It was a giant Dinky toy, come to life.

His toy.

And, there he was. Five years old again. Finding that shoebox full of treasure at the bottom of the carton of kitchen junk his mother had bought for virtually nothing from the charity shop clearance sale. There'd been more than a dozen of the tiny pre-loved metal vehicles but his absolute favourite had been that little red MG roadster, even if it did have chipped paint and a missing wheel. He could almost feel the sharp edges of it in his hand right now, as his fingers curled into a fist—the way they had back then, as they clutched the toy hidden in his pocket, whenever something important was happening. Like when he had to change schools. Or when the big boys on the block were following him home…

Blake dismissed the memory of that fear with a soft snort. His upbringing had had its advantages because he wasn't afraid of anything now.

And this real-life toy wasn't anything like his miniature version. Someone must have spent a fortune restoring it. He'd bet it had a completely new motor now, and that soft, red leather upholstery certainly wasn't original. A new staff member, perhaps? Or a visiting consultant who had the means to indulge a pricey hobby? The idea of spending huge amounts of money purely for pleasure was distasteful but he wasn't going to allow that to tarnish a memory that had been a poignant reminder of something very special. It became so much more muted when you were an adult, that bolt of sheer happiness that life could deliver something so amazing. When you could find real treasure so unexpectedly.

He pulled his helmet off. He was tucking it under his arm when the soft, early morning air around him, still blurred with those long-ago memories, was shattered by a sound that lifted the hairs on the back of his neck.

A scream of pure terror.

'*Help*…oh, God… *Help*…'

It was coming from the adjoining public car park. Blake's helmet bounced, unseen, off the asphalt behind him. He vaulted over the dividing fence with only a touch of his hand to boost him. The heels of his cowboy-style boots beat a tattoo on the hard surface as he ran towards the terrible sound. His peripheral vision caught the movement of others coming in the same direction but he was there first. The young woman standing beside the opened back door of her car didn't appear to be injured or unwell. She just looked petrified.

'What is it? What's happened?'

The question was redundant a split second later, because he could see into the back seat of the car now. Into the baby seat. He could see the blue lips of a baby who wasn't breathing.

The safety harness was already undone and it was easy to lift the infant with his hands under its armpits, his fingers supporting the head. Sometimes, being moved suddenly could be enough to restart breathing but Blake could feel how unresponsive this baby was as he stepped back from the car. He dropped to his knees and cradled the baby in his arms, tilting the head back to ensure the airway was open as he covered the tiny nose and mouth with his lips as he delivered a rescue breath.

And then another. He could see the chest rising so he knew that the airway wasn't obstructed but there was still no response. With two fingers positioned on the centre of the baby's chest he began rapid compressions. A few seconds later, he paused to deliver another two breaths.

Other people had arrived now.

'What happened?'

'How long since he stopped breathing?'

The mother was sobbing. 'I knew there was something wrong, that's why I was bringing him here but I thought he'd...that he'd just fallen asleep... It was just before I turned into the car park...'

'Should I go and get a resus trolley?'

It was a nurse he knew very well who was asking the question. Harriet Collins worked in the intensive care unit but she was also a founding member of the Specialist Disaster Response team that was a big part of Blake's life as well.

Blake had filled the baby's lungs with air again and lifted his head to answer Harriet as he started another set of compressions but then he paused for a second. He could feel the difference beneath his hands. The tension of muscles contracting as the baby took a breath on its own.

And then another.

Blake got to his feet with the baby still in his arms. 'No trolley,' he told Harriet. 'The sooner we get inside the better.'

He was already taking off, heading towards the nearest entrance to the emergency department through the ambulance bay. He could have this baby in their well-equipped resuscitation area in less than a minute if he ran.

He heard the despairing wail of the baby's mother behind him but Harriet was onto it. A swift glance back showed her putting an arm around the still terrified mother's shoulders. 'Come with us,' he heard her say. 'Dr Cooper knows what he's doing, I promise. He's the best...'

He also heard the mother's response.

'But he doesn't even *look* like a doctor...'

'So this is your first day here, dear?'

'Yes, it is, Mrs Henderson.'

'Oh, call me Dottie, dear. Everyone does, you know.'

'Okay, Dottie.'

Samantha Braithwaite smiled at her elderly patient then shifted her gaze to run a practised eye over the drip rate of the IV fluids. She moved the little plastic wheel with her thumb a fraction. The saline drip was only up to keep a vein open—Dottie wasn't hypotensive or dehydrated.

'Is it your first job as a nurse?'

'Oh, no...just my first day here at Bondi Bayside Hospital. I'm very excited.'

'It's a lovely hospital.'

'It is. Maybe you'll get a view of the beach from your room when you're up on the ward. I had a tour a while ago with my friend, Harriet. She works in Intensive Care and she told me about the job coming up here. I couldn't wait to apply for it.'

'It must be a very exciting place to work, here in Emergency. But you're going to see all manner of dreadful things.' Faded blue eyes were full of concern. 'Are you sure that's right for you? I'm sure I couldn't do it.'

Sam's smile was reassuring now. 'I've worked in Emergency for years now, Dottie. At other hospitals in Sydney. I love it. Yes, you can see some dreadful things but it's exciting, too. We get to save lives quite often.'

'And here I am holding up a bed with not an ounce of excitement to offer.'

'You're a treasure.' Sam squeezed Dottie's hand. 'Are you comfortable? I can arrange some more pain relief for you.'

'No...it's fine as long as I don't move. The pillows are helping.' Dottie sighed. 'I can't believe I've been stupid enough to break my hip. You'd think I would have learned to watch my step after ninety-odd years of practice, wouldn't you?'

'These things happen. You're not at all stupid. I'd say you're as bright as a button.'

Sam knew she should be moving on to check patients in the adjoining cubicles that had been assigned to her but she knew they were all low acuity, like the homeless guy who was sleeping off last night's alcohol and the teenager who was being monitored to make sure that his blood sugar levels were stable again. But they had buzzers they could use if they needed assistance urgently and there was something in Dottie's tone that told her how anxious this particular patient was. That she needed more of Sam's attention.

'Is there anyone I can call that could come and keep you company? A family member or a friend?'

'No...my friends are all in the home, now. I'll see them when I get back.'

'Is there anything else I can do to make you more comfortable?'

'A cup of tea would be lovely...and maybe a gingernut?'

'I'm sorry, Dottie. You're nil by mouth at the moment because we're waiting to take you up to Theatre for your operation.'

Yes…that was a flash of real fear in her patient's eyes. Sam squeezed her hand again and this time, she didn't let go.

'I'm quite sure that you'll be fine,' she said quietly. 'It's a straightforward procedure these days. You'll be on your feet in no time.' Her smile widened. 'I wouldn't be surprised if you're dancing again, soon.'

'Oh…we used to love dancing, me and my Bill.'

'Your husband?'

Dottie nodded. 'My third.' She winked at Sam. 'Third time lucky it was, for me. Are you married, dear?'

'No… I'm only twenty-eight.'

'I got married for the first time when I was eighteen.'

'Oh…' Sam widened her eyes. 'Maybe I'm on the shelf, then.'

'No…things are different these days. It's sensible to wait for the right one. I lost my first husband in the war, so that wasn't my fault but the second one was definitely a mistake. I should have kept looking a bit longer.' There was a gleam in Dottie's eyes that suggested she was well distracted from her fear. 'You're such a pretty girl, dear. I'm sure you've got lots of suitors.'

Sam laughed. 'What a lovely, old-fashioned word. I've had a few boyfriends, if that's what you mean. I'm too young to be thinking about getting married. There's too many things I want to do first.'

'Don't wait too long, dear. You might let the right one slip past...'

'I'll keep that in mind. I'd better go now, but I'll be back soon, okay?'

It really was time that Sam checked on her other patients although it was possible that that comment had struck a nerve. Why hadn't she found anyone that turned out to be a contender for the position of the 'right' one? Dottie had been right. With the classic combination of blonde hair and blue eyes, Sam was never short of attracting attention but she'd discovered that being pretty wasn't necessarily an advantage. The interest she attracted tended to be shallow and the end goal blatantly obvious.

'Before you go, dear...do you think you

could bring me a bedpan? I've been dying to have a wee for ages now.'

Sam turned back, the curtain still bunched in her hand. 'Of course, Dottie.' She pulled the curtain closed again. 'There should be one under the bed. Yes, here it is. Let me help you…we need to be careful not to move the pillows supporting your leg.'

With the covered bedpan in her hand, Sam left Dottie's cubicle to head towards the sluice room a few minutes later. She swerved to avoid a phlebotomist and her trolley, which put her in line with the doors to the ambulance bay that were sliding open.

'Move,' someone barked at her.

An alarmed glance showed an unusual scenario. She might have expected uniformed ambulance officers pushing a trolley at speed after a command like that but this was different.

Very different.

A tall man, wearing jeans and cowboy boots, with a tumble of dark wavy hair that reached his shoulders was coming in at almost a run. He had a baby in his arms. People behind him were running to keep up with his long strides. A distraught-looking woman.

And… Harriet? She should be heading upstairs to start her shift in ICU, surely?

Not that she had any time to wonder what was going on. This was clearly a father on a mission to help his sick baby and Sam did, indeed, have to get out of his way. Her long, blonde ponytail swung wildly as she leapt aside—straight into the path of the phlebotomist's trolley. Racks of glass test tubes rattled and toppled to crash to the floor. A box of vacuum tubes followed, to open and spill its contents over a surprisingly large area. Sam herself was knocked off balance. Not enough to fall onto broken glass, fortunately, but it was enough to send the bedpan in her hands flying. Contact with the floor also spilled *its* contents and all Sam could do for a moment was stare in absolute horror, a hand instinctively coming up to cover her gaping mouth.

The noise made heads turn from every direction, including the man who was now past Sam, on his way to one of the major resuscitation areas. She could feel his appalled glare so strongly she had to turn her head and, for a heartbeat, his gaze held hers.

Dark, dark eyes.

An incredulous gaze. As if he simply couldn't

believe that anyone in this department could be so incredibly incompetent. As if his faith in people here being able to help his baby had just been dealt a devastating blow.

And then he was gone.

And there were voices all around Sam.

'Stand back. Stay away from the broken glass.'

'Someone get a mop.'

'I'm sorry. I didn't even *see* you...' The young phlebotomist was looking close to tears.

'It was my fault. I jumped back without looking. I'm so sorry.'

'Just move,' a senior nurse snapped, 'so we can get this mess cleaned up.'

The young technician pulled her trolley clear and muttered something about needing more test tubes as she fled. A member of the domestic staff was already here with a bucket and mop. Sam snatched up the bedpan and kept going towards the sluice room. If nothing else, a quieter space would give her a moment to get over what felt like humiliation.

She couldn't help a sideways glance as she passed the resuscitation area. The curtains weren't completely closed. She could see Harriet in there, with her arm around a sobbing woman. She could see the baby on the bed and staff members busy. Someone had wrapped a tiny blood pressure cuff around an arm and was sliding an oxygen saturation probe onto a finger. Someone else was attaching ECG electrodes. Weirdly, the baby's father—who looked like he'd just come from a gig with his rock band—was standing at the head of the bed, where the person responsible for the airway was supposed to stand. And someone was handing him a stethoscope.

What the heck?

She dropped the disposable bedpan into the rubbish and then turned on the taps over the huge sink to wash her hands. She took her time, using a lot of soap and then paper towels to prolong the process a little longer. Like that young technician, she was fighting an urge to cry.

Her first day on her new job, when all she'd hoped for was to perform well enough to make it obvious that she would be a valuable team member and all she'd done was to make people think she was totally incompetent. Clumsy at best. A liability at worst.

She was an emergency department nurse, for heaven's sake. She should be able to cope with an unfolding crisis in her sleep, not jump like a startled deer just because someone was rushing towards her and barking like a guard dog.

Sam took a deep breath and then lifted her chin.

She had patients assigned to her care and she was going to go back and do her job. And, on her way back, she would apologise to the charge nurse, Emily.

'It was an accident.' Emily actually smiled when Sam spoke to her. 'Unfortunate timing but I saw what happened and I can't blame you for getting a fright. It's not like Blake to speak to people like that but he was under a fair bit of stress. He'd just resuscitated that baby out in the car park.'

'Blake?'

'Blake Cooper. He's one of our top consultants.'

'No way…'

What had been intended as no more than an astonished inward reaction must have escaped as a whisper but Emily didn't seem offended. Her lips twitched.

'I know...but he looks different when he's in his scrubs and has that hair tied up. You'll see...'

Sam didn't want to see. She'd never forget that appalled glance he'd given her. It would have been bad enough if he'd been the baby's father but at least she wouldn't have to see him again. That she'd come to the notice of one of this department's consultants in such a humiliating manner was too much to even try and process right now.

'How's the baby?'

'Stable. Looks like he's got a respiratory infection going on but they're also querying an underlying heart condition. He's on his way to PICU at the moment for monitoring and follow up. Oh...your patient, Mrs Henderson? They're coming to take her to Theatre any minute. She was asking for you. Perhaps you could go up with her?'

'Sure. But what about my other patients?'

'The registrar's discharged the ETOH overdose. And the diabetic lad is eating breakfast. We'll discharge him as soon as his mum gets back with his clothes. Don't worry...' Emily smiled again. 'I'll have a whole new list for you as soon as you get back. I might give you some time in the plaster room. And the paediatric corner—just to let you get a feel for the place.'

Or to keep her out of harm's way?

Sam managed to paste a smile onto her face. 'That'll be great. Thanks.'

What a start to the day.

It was nearly two hours later before Blake Cooper felt like things were back to normal. He had a crisp, clean scrub tunic over his jeans, his penlight torch clipped onto his top pocket along with his pens, and his pager and phone attached to a lower pocket. His hair was neatly combed and fastened into the looped ponytail that was appropriate to his work environment and his own stethoscope lay over his shoulders.

The lasting impression of the dramatic start to his day was an odd mix. There was an enormous relief that the baby was going to be fine. A cardiac abnormality had been ruled out and the respiratory arrest seemed to have been caused by difficulty breathing due to a bad case of bronchiolitis, which was now being treated by the specialist paediatric team. The stress levels had been remarkably high as he was carrying that baby into Emergency, knowing that he could have already stopped breathing again on the journey from the car park but it didn't excuse the way he'd shouted at that nurse who'd been right in his path.

So there was an element of guilt to go with the relief. No wonder the poor girl jumped. He'd never seen her before, either, so maybe she was a relief nurse who wasn't even experienced in being in an often chaotic environment like the ED. The sound of smashing glass had made him think that he might have been responsible for causing a nasty injury but when he'd looked, she was still on her feet and all he could see beneath a halo of very blonde hair and horrified eyes was a face half covered by a hand.

A hand with ridiculously polished nails. Polka dots?

Who the hell put polka dots on their nails? Nobody who was serious about working in a place like this, that was for sure.

Emily was near the triage desk, updating details on the huge board that kept track of the whereabouts and condition of all the patients in this busy emergency department.

'Hey, Em...' Blake paused for a moment. 'Thanks so much for sending someone to rescue my helmet and bag from the car park. Much appreciated.'

'No worries, Blake. You can pay me back by seeing how many of these patients can be discharged. Like this asthma attack in cubicle three. Her oxygen saturation levels have been normal for the last hour but she's anxious. Used her alarm to call an ambulance even before she'd tried her inhaler.'

'I'll go and have a chat.' Blake scanned the rest of the glass board, hoping to find something more challenging but the resuscitation and high acuity areas were currently vacant.

The peal of childish laughter made Blake, and everyone else around him, turn. It was a welcome change from the sounds children usually made here and there were smiles breaking out everywhere as a toddler came towards them at speed, crowing with delight. An adult was in hot pursuit, arms outstretched to catch the escapee.

Hands that were almost in contact with the

small person whose nappy was now loose enough to hamper chubby legs.

Hands that had fingernails with polka dots. *'Gotcha...'*

The toddler didn't seem to mind being captured. With another gurgle of laughter he wrapped his arms around the nurse's neck. She planted a kiss on the curly head and then turned to take him back to where he was supposed to be—presumably the paediatric area. The moment she became aware of her audience was very obvious. Her eyes widened and her smile was fading as she caught her bottom lip between her teeth.

Then her gaze collided with Blake's and a flush of colour instantly stained her cheeks.

And, for the second time in a single day, he was blindsided.

She'd had her face half covered the first time he'd seen her so he hadn't realised...

He hadn't realised that this was the most beautiful woman he'd ever clapped eyes on in his entire life.

Sun-kissed blonde hair and the bluest eyes imaginable. A cute little nose and a generous mouth clearly designed for smiling—or for being kissed...

He couldn't drag his gaze away from her.

She was tall and slim, as well. A model masquerading as a nurse. A Disney princess who probably had a tiara and frothy ball gown tucked away in her locker.

He was still staring as she hurried away with the toddler peering over her shoulder. As if mocking him, a small hand was waving at Blake.

'Oh, dear...' Emily murmured. 'She's not having the best first day, poor thing.'

Blake's inward breath made him realise that he hadn't taken one for a while. 'Who *is* that?'

'Samantha Braithwaite. She's come here from Sydney Central with impeccable references including postgrad qualifications in trauma management.'

There was a moment's silence, then, possibly because Blake's tone had finally filtered through to his colleague.

'Oh, no...' Emily sighed. 'Do I have to warn her of your reputation?'

Blake grinned at her. 'Do I have a reputation?'

She laughed. 'Go away. Do your work. What

you do in your personal life is none of my business.'

He pretended not to hear her final murmur as he headed for cubicle three.

'And thank goodness for that…'

CHAPTER TWO

'Oh, my God, Harriet. I can't go back tomorrow…'

Ignoring the glass of wine her friend had put in front of her, Sam buried her face in her hands.

'Don't be daft. It'll be fine.'

'Everybody thinks I'm an idiot.'

'That's not true and you know it.'

Sam reached for her glass and took a long sip. Okay…maybe not everybody thought that but one person certainly did and he wasn't just one of the senior doctors in her new department and therefore her boss.

He was, quite possibly, the most gorgeous man she'd ever seen in her entire life. Emily had been quite right that Blake Cooper looked different in his scrubs. When she'd seen him later today, thanks to chasing that wayward toddler, his hair was pulled back, sleek against his head, the length of it hidden in a kind of knot at the back. And, without the distraction of those rock god tresses, it was his eyes that grabbed attention. Eyes that were so dark you couldn't distinguish the pupils. Brooding eyes.

Drop dead sexy…

But also capable of delivering a withering glance. As they had, in that first moment he'd noticed her thanks to that unfortunate bedpan incident.

Sam was staring at her glass of wine, now. 'Has it ever occurred to you that chardonnay looks a lot like urine?'

Harriet let out a peal of laughter that made heads turn in this trendy wine bar with its glorious view of the beach.

'Let it go.' She was grinning.

'I can't. I practically threw a full bedpan of the stuff at the feet of one of Bondi Bayside's top emergency consultants. You were there. You must have seen the way he glared at me.'

Pushing her fingers into her hair loosened strands that escaped the coil she had created so carefully in the early hours of this morning. She pulled the clip from the back of her head and let the rest of it escape as well. Maybe that would help her try and move on from her disastrous day.

'I think he had other things on his mind,' Harriet told her. 'Honestly, he'll have forgotten all about it by tomorrow. And, if he hasn't, he'll make a joke about it.'

Sam finally picked up her glass and took a sip. 'Why *were* you there, anyway?'

'I heard someone screaming for help in the car park. And then I saw Blake leaping over the fence like some hero in an action movie. Joining in was automatic—it was like a training exercise for the team or something.'

'But you don't work in ED.'

'I mean the SDR. I've told you all about that. Wasn't it one of the reasons you wanted to come and work on this side of town?'

Sam nodded. She'd long been envious of Harriet's involvement with the Specialist Disaster Response team. How exciting would it be to get dispatched as a first response to major incidents like floods or fires or an avalanche, maybe? To be working in the field facing the kind of challenges that you'd never experience in a nice, safe emergency department. She fully intended to try and join the team herself and, given that she wasn't a fire-fighter or a paramedic, the first step in that ambition had been to become a member of Bondi Bayside Hospital's staff.

Her heart had just sunk a little, however. Had Harriet just made her aware of a possible fly in the ointment? A fly the size of an albatross?

'Blake's in the SDR?'

'Are you kidding? It was pretty much his baby right from the start. He told me once that he'd been planning to join Médecins Sans Frontières. He'd been through the selection process and was just waiting for his first posting but then his mum had a stroke and she's pretty dependent on him now so he couldn't go anywhere. He had a mate in the fire service who got him into USAR and that's when he came up with the idea of a medical team that could add another level of skill to a first response.'

'USAR?'

'Urban Search and Rescue. I've done a course myself. You learn how to find victims in situations like collapsed buildings. It's awesome. I think most firies do it and a lot of paramedics. Not so many doctors or nurses but it's attracting more interest now. You have to do it if you're in the team. Blake's actually one of the regional instructors now. Plus, he's winch-trained for helicopters. I'm thinking of doing that training myself, actually. Bit scary, though…'

Sam was nodding but her thoughts were skidding off in another direction. Blake Cooper was getting more intriguing with everything she heard about him. He was obviously a born leader. He wasn't afraid of danger.

And he loved his mother.

He was also clearly at the top of the SDR ladder.

'Um… Who gets to decide if someone's allowed to join the team?'

'There's a committee. People have their names put forward by someone who's already on the team and there's a discussion and a vote to see if they're going to be invited to a training session to try out. And then there's another vote to decide whether they get to join.' Harriet raised her eyebrows. 'Want me to put *your* name forward?'

'Sure. But, if Blake gets to vote, I think I might have killed my chances.'

'By throwing a bedpan at him?'

'It wasn't just that. He saw me later today, too. Chasing down a toddler who'd taken off from the paediatric area. He must think I'm totally incompetent.'

She knew that for a fact, thanks to the second time they had made eye contact today. The moment the chase had ended when she'd scooped up that adorable little boy, she could feel the intensity of his gaze. And his expression…well, the only interpretation she could put on it was complete incredulity. As if he couldn't believe what he was seeing—that she was still working in his department?

Harriet shrugged. 'He'll soon find out you're not. He's one of the smartest guys I know and he can read people pretty well. I could tell him myself, just to speed up the process.'

'No, don't do that, Harry. It feels like I'd be trying to get something the easy way. Breaking some unwritten rule for a team that must have to rely on everyone being super competent. I'll just have to impress him at work somehow, if I get the chance. And *then* you could put my name forward.'

'Don't try too hard,' Harriet advised. 'He

likes to make his own decisions. If he gets pushed he's likely to walk off and do his own thing. He's a…what's the word for it…when someone's a law unto themselves kind of thing?'

'Fascinating' was the first word that sprang to mind. Or maybe 'irresistible'…

'Maverick, that's it.' Harriet's nod was satisfied.

'Hmm… I guess he is. I mean, that *hair*…'

'I know. Not my thing but it doesn't seem to put other girls off.'

'And he was still wearing jeans under that scrubs top. And…and *cowboy* boots?'

Harriet was laughing again. 'I guess when you're that brilliant at what you do, you can get away with pretty much anything. He's a nice guy, Sam. As long as you don't get too close.'

'Oh? What happens if you do?'

'Well, you don't. That's just it. You get a broken heart, that's all. Oh…speaking of hearts.' Harriet glanced at her watch. 'I've got to run. Pete's taking me out to dinner and that doesn't happen very often. I *think*…' She bit her lip, hazel eyes sparkling beneath her tumble of auburn curls. 'I think he's going to ask me to move in with him.'

'Really?' Oh, my God, Harry. That's almost a proposal. Are you going to say yes?'

Harriet grinned. 'You have *met* Pete, haven't you?'

'Of course I have.'

She'd met Harriet's boyfriend more than once. A tall, very fit fireman who was also part of the SDR, Pete had sun-bleached blond hair thanks to his favourite hobby of surfing and a body that was a testament to the number of hours he spent at the gym. He was undeniably good looking and seemed like a perfectly nice guy but...

Sam gave her head a tiny shake as she reached for her bag. There was no 'but'. Her parents would be rapt if she brought someone like Pete home. They would be horrified if she turned up with someone like...

Like Blake Cooper.

Good grief...one glass of wine on a sunny afternoon and it had gone straight to her head, hadn't it?

'I hope Pete takes you somewhere really romantic.'

'I don't care if it's a fast food joint, to be honest. You coming to the bus stop?'

'No. I left my car at work.' She hugged her friend. 'And I've got some shopping to do. Catch you tomorrow, maybe?'

Luckily there was a pharmacy in the group of local shops near the wine bar. Sam headed in and grabbed an item that had been at the back of her mind all day.

Nail polish remover.

The little red car was still there.

Blake Cooper was finally heading home after a long shift. He had already worked more than his allocated hours and he would have stayed longer still so that he'd had a chance to get up to the paediatric wing and check on the baby he'd resuscitated this morning but he had another place he needed to be and some-one who needed him to be there.

It made him smile to see the car again. He'd have to tell his mum about it, he de-cided, as he climbed onto his bike and rocked it free of its stand. A trip down memory lane for both of them was one of her favourite things. Maybe he'd even have a dig in those old boxes at the back of the garage and see if that box of toys was still there somewhere.

His smile died as he lifted his head to put his helmet on.

No way…

It couldn't be…

But it was. The woman walking towards the little red car was none other than the new nurse from ED.

Samantha Braithwaite.

The name had burned itself into his memory banks instantly, with a similar lightning bolt kind of finality as what she looked like.

And, if he'd thought she was the most beautiful woman he'd ever seen in that moment, it paled in comparison to what he was seeing now.

She'd been wearing scrubs then. With her hair no more than a lumpy knot at the back of her head.

Right now, she was wearing a gypsy-style, loose white blouse and faded denim shorts with frayed hems that showed off an incredible length of slim, bronzed legs. And her hair… Released from that knot, it was astonishingly long, reaching her waist in a fall of gentle waves that the summer evening breeze was playing with.

Forget the impression of being a princess or a model. What Blake was looking at now was more like an image from one of those magazines he'd hidden under his bed as a teenager.

Every man's fantasy.

And she owned the vintage MG roadster? Apparently so, given that she'd climbed inside and was now rolling the soft top back.

Blake's breath came out in a snort. Of course she did. It was probably a gift from a rich father. Or husband. A boyfriend at the very least. Women who looked like that were never alone in life.

Maybe she'd had those stupid dots painted on her nails to match its paintwork, even.

This was ridiculous. Why was he even giving this woman and her questionable life choices any head space at all? Blake jammed his helmet onto his head and kicked the engine of his bike into life. He took off with perhaps a bit more acceleration than was strictly necessary so it really shouldn't have surprised him that she turned her head to stare at him.

What did come as a surprise was that he rather liked the idea that she was watching him.

'How long will I have to wait?'

'I'm not sure, Jess.' Sam had come into one of the cubicles assigned to her on this shift, to do the obs on a patient who'd been brought into the ED by ambulance earlier this morning. She watched the drip rate of the IV fluids and slowed them a little by turning the small wheel on the line. These fluids were running simply to keep a vein open in case medication was needed at some point. 'I can make a call and try and find out, if you like?'

She knew which of the phones on the main desk she could use. And who to call. After a week in her new department, Sam was comfortably familiar with where things were, subtle differences in protocols and her new group of colleagues, both in the department and the consultants who got called in. They were a great bunch of people and Sam knew she was going to make new friends here. She particularly liked Kate Mitchell, an O&G surgeon, who was apparently also a member of the SDR team although she hadn't had a chance to talk to her about it yet. She lived in the same apartment building as Harriet so maybe she should suggest that they all meet up for a drink one evening, or something.

'That would be great.' Jess nodded. 'I've let them know at work that I'm going to be late but I haven't worked there that long, you know? I don't want them to think I'm a liability.'

'I get it. I'm pretty new here, myself. Let me just do your blood pressure and things and I'll get on it.'

At twenty-five, Jess was only a few years younger than Sam so she already felt an affinity with this patient. That she wanted to impress people at a new job gave them another connection. Sam smiled at her as she wrapped the blood pressure cuff around her arm. Not that she'd managed to impress anybody here yet, as far as she was aware, but at least she'd been able to keep her head down and work hard and had, thank goodness, avoided calling attention to herself for any less than desirable incidents.

She still felt like she was on probation, however, whenever Blake Cooper was in the near vicinity. Which seemed to be an awful lot of the time. She'd developed a kind of internal radar that alerted her to his presence in the department, even when he wasn't visible, which was a bit weird but she'd proved herself correct often enough to trust it now. It was like some kind of energy that gave a recognisable crackle to the atmosphere.

She wasn't into auras or anything like that, but it wasn't hard to recognise charisma and she'd already been intrigued by this man. When she'd seen him roar off on his motorbike that evening last week, the jolt of what could only be described as pure lust had been shocking enough to explain the crackle she was now so aware of. It was also the reason she was avoiding eye contact with him at all costs. It wasn't easy, either, because that feeling of being on probation came from the knowledge that he was keeping an eye on her.

Watching what she was up to and whether she was doing her job to an acceptable level of expertise.

How embarrassing would it be if he could see how attractive she found him?

She noted a normal blood pressure and then picked up the tympanic thermometer.

'I'm sure I don't have a temperature,' Jess told her. 'I don't feel sick.'

'We're just keeping an eye on things. An infection is one of the things that could be interfering with your anti-epileptic medication.'

'I don't even think I had a seizure. I just fainted or something.'

'You may as well get checked out properly while you're here.'

'I wouldn't *be* here, if that cop hadn't been in the coffee shop when it happened. He was the one who called an ambulance.'

'I might have done the same thing myself, if I'd noticed your MedicAlert bracelet.'

'But I was fine by the time it arrived. If he hadn't threatened to call my parents if I didn't go to the hospital, I'd be at work now and wouldn't be here wasting people's time.'

'When was the last time you had an EEG?'

'After my last seizure, nearly two years ago. Oh…' Jess groaned. 'I was just about to be able to get my driver's licence back, you know? This really sucks…'

'I know.' Sam wrote the normal temperature onto the chart. 'It's a bit stressful starting a new job. Have you been sleeping okay? Eating well?'

They were all questions that had been asked by the junior registrar who'd been assigned this patient but, sometimes, people found it less intimidating to chat to their nurse and new information could be forthcoming.

But Jess just shook her head. 'You're starting to sound like my mother.'

'Sorry.' Sam grinned. 'Helicopter parent, huh? I know what that's like.'

'You'd think I was still six years old, not a responsible adult.' Jess sighed heavily, leaning her head back on her pillows. 'I don't blame them, you know? My brother died in a car accident when he was seventeen. They've been watching me like a hawk ever since and I know how much they care. That's why I can't let them know I'm in here. My mother would totally panic.'

Sam had frozen for a moment, after clipping the chart back onto the end of the bed.

'I understand,' she said quietly.

Man...she had way more in common with this patient than an age group or a new job.

'And I'm so sorry to hear about your brother. That's really rough.'

She knew exactly how rough. Not that her

brother had died in a car crash. No. Alistair had been feeding his adrenaline addiction and climbing a mountain. He'd been twenty-five. Sam had only been sixteen and the loss of her only brother and her best friend had been devastating. Her parents were never going to get over it.

'It wasn't his fault. They said it was, because he was driving but I don't believe it. One of his mates in the car said he collapsed at the wheel but he'd had a head injury and nobody believed him.'

There were tears rolling down Jess's face. 'It changed everything, you know? It was when I had my first seizure and knew how terrified my parents were. We all miss him... *so* much...'

Jess was sobbing now. Sam moved to put her arms around her patient. She needed to comfort her. Emotional distress like this wasn't going to help. It could even possibly trigger another seizure.

And, even as the thought appeared, she could feel the sudden change within her arms. The instant lack of any muscle tension.

'Jess? *Jess...?*'

The lack of any response was no surprise.

Swiftly, Sam removed the pillows from behind Jess's head and tilted her chin to ensure her airway was open before pressing
her fingers to her neck to check her pulse.
The sudden jerking beneath her hand made
it impossible to feel anything. All she could
do now was to make sure that she kept Jess
safe for the duration of this seizure. And to
alert the registrar, Sandra, of this new de-
velopment.

The movements weren't violent enough to
put Jess in danger of falling off the bed so
Sam took a quick step back to flick the curtain open far enough to call whoever was
closest and ask them to find Sandra urgently.

There was only one person close enough
to call.

And this was not an appropriate moment
to avoid eye contact.

Oddly, she didn't need to utter a word.

And, even more oddly, it felt like she'd
known that since the first time she had made
eye contact with this extraordinary man. It
was exactly why she'd been avoiding this—it
felt like he could see anything that she might
be trying to hide.

Not that she was trying to hide anything

right now. She needed back-up and it took only a split second. With two strides, Blake was behind the curtain with her, his intense gaze on Jess as he took in the uncontrolled movements of her body.

'This is Jess, twenty-five years old,' Sam told him rapidly. 'History of epilepsy. She was brought in by ambulance nearly an hour ago and is waiting for an EEG. She…um…got upset when we were talking. Sudden loss of consciousness and the seizure started maybe fifteen seconds later.'

'Draw up some midazolam,' Blake ordered. 'Five milligrams. We're going to need it if this lasts more than five minutes. Grab some valproate as well, in case the midaz isn't enough.'

Sam's hands were rock steady as she swiftly found the ampoules, double checked the name, dose and expiry date with Blake and drew up the drugs.

He checked his watch. 'Three minutes,' he murmured. He was resting his hand on the arm that had the IV line inserted, to protect it from being knocked out of place. 'What was she upset about?'

'She was telling me about her brother who

died in a car crash when he was a teenager. Her epilepsy got diagnosed not long after that.'

'Oh?' Blake slanted a glance towards Sam and, again, there was a moment of communication that went beyond the words being spoken. They both found this snippet of information interesting.

'Apparently, one of the passengers in the car thought he might have collapsed suddenly at the wheel.'

Blake's glance sharpened with what looked like curiosity.

'What are you thinking?'

A lot of people wouldn't have jumped in with both feet the way Sam did. She was a nurse. It wasn't her place to suggest that a doctor's diagnosis might have been wrong. But maybe she recognised the significance of something others might have dismissed and she had the feeling that Blake was on the same wavelength.

'What if it's not epilepsy at all?' Sam suggested quietly. 'But something like long QT syndrome?'

Surprise replaced curiosity in that dark

gaze. 'What do you know about long QT syndrome?'

'It's a delayed repolarisation of the heart that can lead to episodes of *torsades de pointes* and can cause fainting, seizures and sudden death due to ventricular fibrillation. It can be hereditary and run in families.'

'She must have had ECGs done.'

'They did a twelve lead in the ambulance this morning. It was reported as sinus rhythm and NAD.'

No abnormalities detected.

Blake checked his watch again but Sam could see that the drugs weren't going to be needed. The chaotic movements of Jess's body were subsiding. She could see their patient's chest heave as she took a deep breath. Blake quickly turned her into the recovery position, talking quietly as he did so.

'It's okay, Jess,' he said gently. He pulled up the bed cover and tucked it around her shoulders. 'You're fine. Everything's okay. Just rest for a minute.'

Then he straightened. 'Where's that ECG?'

Sam took the manila folder from where it was clipped behind the observations chart she had been filling in a short time ago. The sheet of pink graph paper was behind the ambulance officer's report form. She handed it to Blake and he stared at it for a long minute.

Sam waited, holding her breath, but he didn't say anything. Instead, he handed the trace to her.

'What do *you* think?'

Her mouth went suddenly dry. All aspects of cardiology were fascinating to her but she was no expert and traces were difficult to read. Then she let her breath out slowly. She didn't need to analyse every lead on this ECG. All she needed to look at was the rhythm strip at the bottom and to remember what the normal interval between the downward Q spike and the end of the T wave was. She started counting the tiny squares, the figure of ten being in her head.

'Eight, nine…ten…' She was whispering aloud. 'Eleven…no, it could be twelve.' Her gaze flicked up from the paper. Was she making an idiot of herself, here?

'Hard to tell without a ruler, isn't it?' Blake's gaze was steady. He wasn't looking surprised any more. And curiosity was long gone. This look had a very different message.

He looked seriously impressed.

'Definitely long.' One side of his mouth curled up just a fraction. Okay, maybe there was a bit of surprise mixed into that lingering look. He hadn't expected this from her, had he?

She had wanted a chance to impress him but it was kind of annoying that he *was* so impressed that she might have a brain. Blake Cooper might be the hottest thing on two legs she'd ever met but his attitude was less than desirable. It wasn't the first time that Sam had encountered a reaction that suggested she didn't look as smart as she was. What usually followed was the impression that the fact that she could think was just an added bonus that wasn't particularly relevant.

The burning fuse of the potent attraction she'd been so aware of had just been doused with a bucket of cold water and, ironically, in the moment of realising she didn't have to avoid eye contact with this man any more, it became remarkably easy to break it. She turned towards her patient who was waking up properly now.

But Blake had turned as well and they both reached to take Jess's pulse at the same time.

Skin brushed on skin and Sam had to snatch her hand away as if she'd been burnt.

It *felt* like she'd been burnt.

Maybe that fuse hadn't been extinguished as well as she'd thought.

Blake didn't seem to have noticed anything. 'Give Cardiology a call, would you, Sam?' he asked. 'And bring a monitor when you come back. Hopefully this isn't going to happen again, but it would be helpful to be able to record it if it does.'

'Good call, mate.' Luc Braxton paused by the central desk in the ER to talk to Blake. 'I was having lunch with one of the cardiology team and they told me all about your case. Sounds like you probably saved that young woman's life.'

Blake couldn't take all the credit. He couldn't actually take any of it.

'It was a good call,' he agreed. 'She could well have gone on being treated for epilepsy that didn't exist and died from a VF arrest down the track.'

'You should write the case history up for a journal,' Luc suggested.

'I think it's been done,' Blake said. 'What

bothers me is that nobody queried whether her seizures could have been due to oxygen deprivation in the first place. And I can't really take the credit...' He lifted his gaze to scan the emergency department. 'It was actually one of our nurses who joined the dots.'

'Wow. That's impressive. Who was it?'

'Samantha...someone. She's new.'

'Ah...' Luc raised an eyebrow. 'The one that looks like a model?'

'Mmm.' The response was meant to be discouraging. He didn't want to find out that any of his colleagues found her attractive. And he certainly didn't want to give anyone the impression that he did. She wasn't his type and never would be.

'Give her a pat on the back then.' Luc turned away but then threw a grin over his shoulder. 'Figuratively, I mean.'

Blake ignored the subtle reference to his reputation with women but the suggestion had already been made by the cardiology team. 'I'll do that.'

Not that he could see Sam anywhere. After a week of being so aware of her in the department, half expecting her to do something else that was clumsy or inappropriate, it was a little disconcerting to realise he might have to go looking for her to pass on the congratulations.

Maybe that had something to do with the impression he'd been left with that she hadn't exactly been thrilled to have him take over Jess's management until the patient was transferred to the cardiology department. She'd barely spoken to him when she'd brought the monitor back and busied herself attaching electrodes and then she'd faded into the background when Jess asked her to contact her parents and let them know what was going on.

What had he done to offend her?

And why did it bother him, anyway?

Okay, maybe she'd ditched those frivolous nails but she still belonged to a world he did his best to avoid. A supermodel clone who drove around in a real-life Dinky toy and had the time and inclination to sit around in beauty salons.

The fact that she was intelligent made no difference.

The jolt of electricity he'd felt when his hand had brushed hers shouldn't make any difference, either.

But it did, dammit.

Against his better judgement, Blake had to admit that he was lying to himself by pretending he wasn't attracted to this newcomer.

He was. Seriously attracted.

Not that he was going to act on it.

So, maybe it wasn't a bad thing if he'd somehow offended her. A useful insurance policy if his body decided it would be worth overriding his better judgement and he was tempted to find out if Samantha Braithwaite was single. Or interested.

And why would she be interested anyway? He didn't sit around in wine bars or treat his dates to great seats for some show at the Sydney Opera House. His spare time was devoted to helping out the less privileged members of society at the free clinic and keeping up with any DIY or gardening at his mother's house. And training, of course. If it wasn't an organised session with the SDR team, he'd be out running or at the gym using the climbing wall or something. Physical kind of stuff for the most part.

The kind that made you sweaty and dirty.

Could break your nails, even.

Nope. She definitely wasn't his type.

And he didn't need to go and find Sam. He'd see her soon enough and he could pass on the message.

Or he could write a note and leave it under the windscreen wiper of the car he couldn't help looking for every day when he arrived at work. Except that she'd think it was a ticket or something, wouldn't she? She might be really annoyed by a gesture like that.

Blake thought about that for a moment. Then he turned to Emily who was working nearby at the central desk.

'Got a bit of scrap paper, Em?'

CHAPTER THREE

THE SUN WAS low enough in the sky that Blake had to shield his eyes as he walked through the car park. He almost didn't see the figure standing beside the little red car.

No. Not exactly standing. Samantha Braithwaite had one hip resting on the bonnet, close to one of the headlights. She looked like she was waiting for something. The roof of the car was down so maybe she was waiting for the interior to cool off?

He had to walk past her to get to his bike. It would have been rude not to acknowledge her, so he nodded.

She nodded back.

'I got your note.'

Blake's steps slowed. Uh-oh…

He'd left that note a couple of days ago. He'd had a day off the next day and he'd barely seen her today with the department having been so busy so he'd forgotten that it could have been annoying. That she might have thought she was getting a ticket for parking in the wrong place or something.

But Sam was smiling now. 'Thanks,' she said. 'It was nice to know that someone was impressed but…'

Blake had stopped walking. He raised an eyebrow.

'But how did you know this was my car?'

Oh, man… She had been waiting for something, hadn't she?

She'd been waiting for *him*.

He shrugged. 'It's a distinctive car. I saw you getting into it. On your first day here, I think it was.'

She slid off the car. The way she caught the length of her hair and pushed it back over her shoulder came across as a defensive gesture. An understandable one, perhaps, and Blake felt a slight twinge of remorse. He hadn't intended to remind her of the humiliating incident of dropping a bedpan in front of everyone.

'Fair enough. And you ride a Ducati.'

His eyebrow still hadn't lowered. Maybe

because he remembered that she'd been watching him ride away that day. That he'd revved a bit more than necessary.

That he'd liked that she was watching him.

Dangerous territory, here. It would be oh, so easy to keep talking. To flirt with her a little, even. He willed his muscles to tense, ready to keep moving forward. Oddly, they weren't co-operating.

'That's right.'

'Seven-fifty Sport, I believe.'

Good grief. She knew about bikes? His eyebrow had dropped now. His jaw probably had as well.

'My brother was into bikes.'

'Ah.' Past tense. 'So he grew out of his wilder inclinations, then?'

Sam seemed to have found an interesting oil stain on the asphalt. 'Something like that.'

It was time for him to move. To wish his new colleague a good evening and then go and get on with what was left of his own.

'So...do you know what happened? To Jess, I mean. The girl with the long QT syndrome?'

'She was kept in for some tests but I expect she's been discharged by now.'

'I meant her management. Did she get put on beta blockers? Or is an implantable defibrillator on the cards?'

So she'd been waiting for him just because she wanted follow-up on a case they'd both been involved with?

Very professional but a bit odd to be doing it in the car park when she could have approached him at work at any time. Usually, if women went out of their way to talk to him, they had a very different agenda in mind.

Sam didn't wait for him to respond. 'I guess it depends on the genotype and the exact QT interval when it's been corrected for things like gender and age.'

'Yeah... You got it.' A warning bell was ringing somewhere in the back of Blake's mind. Sam clearly wanted to keep this conversation going.

She wanted...something...

He actually took a step forward to suggest that he had someplace else he needed to be. It could go two ways. Either she'd take the hint and give up or she'd reveal what it was that was really on her mind.

It appeared that Sam could ignore hints.

'Can I ask you something?'

'Sure.'

'I'm friends with Harriet Collins. From ICU?'

'Yeah… I know Harry.'

'She'd told me about the Specialist Disaster Response team. I heard all about that last callout you had, to that bushfire?'

Blake waited politely for the question he was supposed to answer but Sam seemed to be searching for what she wanted to say.

'And?' he prompted.

The movement of her chest as she took a deep breath caught his eye. That hint of cleavage in the low scoop of her T-shirt was even more eye-catching. He looked away swiftly.

'And it's the sort of thing I'd really like to be able to do myself. To be somewhere on the front line, in a crisis. To be part of an emergency response when it really counts. When it can be a matter of life or death.'

If he'd wanted to flirt with her, this was an ideal opportunity. He could make himself look pretty good by sharing a few war stories, too, if it went that far.

But it wasn't going to go that far.

It wasn't going to go anywhere at all.

'You get that yourself. We get plenty of life or death situations in ED.'

'But it's not the same. We've got any amount of backup and resources in ED. It's…'

There was a frown line between Sam's eyes as, again, she tried to find the words that would explain exactly what she meant.

She didn't need to explain because Blake understood perfectly well. Working in a well-equipped emergency department wasn't as exciting. Or challenging. You didn't have to dig deep and find out what you, as an individual, were really made of.

But he didn't want to get into a discussion that could turn personal very quickly.

So he lifted both eyebrows this time. 'Boring?' he suggested.

'*No*… I love my job. But I'd like the challenge of being able to do more. I really admire what you guys do.'

Blake was silent. Was she hitting on him? No. He knew what a woman looked like when that was happening. Sam's gaze was too steady.

Determined, even.

'So that's what I wanted to ask you. How can I join?'

'*What*?' He hadn't seen this coming.

'I'd really like the opportunity to join the SDR team.'

His breath came out in a startled huff. It was only in the silence that followed that he realised it could have sounded a lot like a bark of laughter.

Sam was standing very still. She hadn't broken the eye contact and he saw the flicker of uncertainty that gave way to a flash of something like anger.

'That's *funny*?'

'No… Sorry, I just wasn't expecting you to say that.'

'Why not?'

No. Maybe it wasn't anger. The bright spots of colour on Sam's cheeks suggested embarrassment. Or possibly humiliation? She had been waiting out here for probably quite some time, given that her shift would have finished ages ago and she had done so in order to ask about something that, inexplicably, she obviously felt quite passionate about.

And he had all but laughed at her.

Now he remembered that moment of connection, when he'd known exactly what she was talking about in wanting the extra dimension of dealing with emergencies when you were a long way away from the relatively safe environment of a hospital department.

He was being a bastard, wasn't he?

But the thought of having Sam in the SDR was...

Well, it was unthinkable, that's what it was.

It was distracting enough to have her in his emergency department. Imagine if she was there during team meetings or on training days? They might be serious sessions but they were also the best of times for Blake. Downtime that fed his need for adventure.

For freedom.

And what if Sam was there during a real callout? They were intense enough situations as it was. A simmering attraction could easily explode into something else. He'd seen that happen before, with Harriet and that firie, Pete, who'd joined the team last year. They were a serious item now, despite everyone knowing how he felt about relationships between team members. He'd actually heard a rumour that they had moved in together recently.

Blake was confident that it wasn't going to happen to him but he wasn't about to make it any more difficult to resist temptation. Because he *was* tempted. Of course he was. He just knew how messy it would get. Girls like Sam didn't go for casual relationships that were only ever intended to be fun for a while. She was the type who would expect champagne dinners, dancing to slow music and a misty proposal down the track that involved a diamond the size of a rock.

But what could he say? That he couldn't have her on the team because any man in the vicinity wouldn't be able to concentrate on the job they were there to do? She might guess that he was talking about himself. But he couldn't really say that she wasn't suitable because she might be worried about breaking a nail without sounding ridiculously sexist.

As his thoughts flashed past in the blink of an eye, Blake involuntarily lowered his gaze to her hands. Those absurd polka dots might have vanished but they were still beautifully manicured nails. On the ends of long, delicate fingers that looked far more suited to playing a piano or arranging flowers than sifting through rubble or messing with ropes.

He didn't like being a bastard, though. He needed to let her down gently.

'Sorry,' he said again. 'It's great that you're interested but...we kind of have a full team at the moment. How 'bout I let you know if we're on the lookout for someone in the future? If you're still interested, we can talk about it then.'

'Sure.' The word was no more than a slightly disappointed monosyllable. Or maybe it was more the sound of someone who knew they were being brushed off. Sam was turning away. Getting into her car. She shot him a quick glance after starting the engine.

'I will be,' she added. And this time her tone was even. Resolute. 'Still interested, that is.'

He'd *laughed* at her.

Worse, he'd brushed her off as not being worth bothering with.

He was going to let her know if they needed someone new? Yeah...like *that* was going to happen...

She'd waited out there in the car park for over an hour hoping to get the chance to talk to him privately. She'd been nervous about it, too. She knew it was probably too soon to say anything but that note that had been left on her car had been an unexpected opportunity she hadn't wanted to waste. Not only had they connected professionally thanks to that long QT syndrome case but he now knew she wasn't incompetent.

So did everybody else. For once, the kind of gossip that went around a hospital department like wildfire had been welcome. Other consultants like Kate Mitchell had taken the time to talk to her about it and say how impressed they'd been and surely Blake must have been pleased that at least one of the cardiologists at Bondi Bayside had complimented one of his department's staff.

But it hadn't made any difference, had it? That look of incredulity on his face when she'd said she wanted to join the team hadn't been all that dissimilar to the look he'd given her when she'd dropped the bedpan in front of him on her first day.

A sound almost like a growl escaped Sam's lips. He'd managed to slide in a reference to that in their brief conversation as well.

It should be enough to quell any interest she had in joining the SDR and make her want to stay as far away as possible from anything that Dr Cooper was involved with.

It was, in fact, doing the opposite. Harriet had been quite correct in reminding her that the idea of being able to join this team had been the major factor in deciding to change hospitals. Blake Cooper wasn't the only person who could help her achieve her goal. She could talk to Luc Braxton, an emergency physician who was involved with the team. Or Kate, for that matter. Maybe she should have done that when they'd been talking about Jess's case.

She hit a number on her Bluetooth speed dial.

'Harry? What are you up to at the moment?'

'Not much. I'm clearing out a shelf in the bathroom for Pete. We decided that it was a much better idea for him to move in here than the other way around because I'm so much closer to the beach.' There was a thump as something got dropped or shifted. 'I have no idea how I collect so many bottles of stuff that never get used. What's up?'

'That committee you told me about—the one that decides whether someone gets to try out for the SDR team—does it have to be a unanimous decision?'

'I have no idea. Why?'

Sam could hear more shuffling sounds and the odd clunk as she relayed the conversation she'd just had. Clearly, Harriet was multitasking and still cleaning out her cupboard.

'It's not true, is it? You don't have too many people on the team at the moment?'

'No. We're always open to new members, as far as I know. It might only be a small team that gets deployed on a callout but you need a lot more people available because not everyone can just walk out of their jobs at a moment's notice. You might have firies tied up at a major fire or a surgeon who's in the middle of an operation or something. That's happened more than once to Kate Mitchell. Everyone has a pager but only the people who can respond will answer. The co-ordinator picks the team according to the different skill sets they have on offer at the time so everything gets covered as best they can.'

'Yeah, I thought it worked something like that. He is trying to put me off, isn't he?'

'I dunno. Doesn't sound like Blake.'

'So who should I talk to next, do you think? Kate? Or Luc?'

'Hmm. I wouldn't do the rounds just yet. Might make you look desperate.'

'Maybe I *am* desperate. I really want this, Harry.'

'Give it a bit of time. Show him that you're serious.'

'How?' Sam took the next exit from the motorway and noted the slow traffic ahead with dismay. Her parents were expecting her for dinner and she was going to be late. She'd have to call them, next, so they wouldn't start worrying.

'Um, maybe you could learn to abseil? That's a really valuable skiil.'

Sam groaned. 'Imagine how much that would freak my parents out. I haven't even been near a climbing wall in a gym since… well, you know.'

'Oh…yeah… I almost forgot. Sorry.'

'It's okay. Joining the SDR is going to freak them out as well but I'm not going to let it stop me. I've been wrapped up in cotton wool for far too long. Maybe that's why I want this so much.'

'Yeah…they can't expect to keep you in cotton wool for ever.'

'It's not that they've tried to. It was my choice to start with because I didn't want them to worry and it just became a way of life. It's felt wrong for a long time but I couldn't find a way to change things. Joining the SDR would do that and I'm sure they would understand why I want to do it so much.'

'You could do a course in disaster management,' Harriet suggested. 'It's actually a university degree now, did you know that? You could do it online. Part time.'

'That would take *years*.'

'It would show commitment, though.'

'I need a faster way to show that I'm serious.'

Sam heard a click that sounded like a cupboard closing. Or maybe it was Harriet snapping her fingers.

'I've got it. Do one of those basic USAR courses. An introductory one. That only takes a weekend.'

'Now that's a really good idea. Where do they happen?'

'I did one here but they don't happen that often. I think they have them all over the country, though. Go online and have a look.'

'Thanks, Harry. You're a star. I'd better let you go. I need to call the folks and let them know that the traffic's holding me up and I haven't been squished in a car accident or something.'

Harriet laughed but Sam could almost see her shaking her head. 'They're never going to get over it, are they?'

'No. And I can't blame them for that.'

She wouldn't be able to blame them for being appalled at her desire to join a team of people who threw themselves into dangerous situations like floods or earthquakes or a plane crash.

Having parked in a leafy street in one of Sydney's most exclusive suburbs, Sam killed the engine of her little car and closed her eyes for a moment as she let out a long sigh.

It wasn't just Blake Cooper who presented an obstacle to what she'd set her heart on but the big difference was that she loved her parents. After so many years of protecting them from further worry, she wasn't able to become the rebel and just do what she wanted no matter if it hurt them.

This was going to take some careful management but she was confident it was doable. And, as soon as she got home this evening, she was going to go online and see what she could find out about the urban search and rescue training courses.

Blake clicked on a shortcut link on the iPad he always carried in his satchel, which was now propped up on the windowsill above his mother's kitchen bench.

He didn't check in nearly as often these days. And it didn't seem to instil quite the same level of yearning, either.

The Australian branch of Médecins Sans Frontières was currently helping to deal with a meningitis epidemic in West Africa, an outbreak of cholera in Yemen and providing surgical teams in Iraq amongst a dozen or more projects scattered over the more troubled areas of the globe. Headlines told him that a nurse had been evacuated from Africa with a serious case of dengue fever and a hospital in the Middle East had been bombed. Casualties included several MSF staff, two of whom were doctors.

It could have been him, Blake mused, if his mother hadn't had that stroke. He would have been out there now, probably having moved from one project to another, with nothing more than a quick visit home once or twice a year. With another click, he went back to the music he was streaming and turned back to the task in hand. He drained the pot of boiled potatoes, added some butter and milk and set about mashing them.

He would have died doing something he was passionate about—helping the least fortunate members of the human population—but that wouldn't have made it any easier for his mother to have coped with, would it? And how unfair would that have been for a woman who'd devoted her life to doing her utmost under challenging circumstances to give her only child the best chance of happiness and success.

He spooned the mashed potato over the savoury mix of meat and vegetables in the baking dish, sprinkled grated cheese on top and slid the pan into a hot oven. Then he scrolled down the rest of the headlines of the news bulletin he'd opened online.

He hadn't given up on the ambition to join MSF, of course, and times like this, confined within the four walls of a tiny bungalow in one of Sydney's sprawling outer suburbs, the sharp teeth of frustration would snap at his heels again. It was the flipside of the coin that represented freedom, wasn't it?

An ordinary little house in the suburbs. A wife and kids and a mortgage.

Trapped for life.

A nightmare for anyone who'd dreamed of freedom since he was old enough to understand how limited the choices in life could be for those less fortunate than others.

Searching for, and buying this house had made him break out in a cold sweat, more than once, even though he would never be living here. This house had been his mum's dream. Her own house, with no threat of being evicted or having to put up with the substandard living conditions of something like a blocked toilet because the landlord couldn't be bothered dealing with it. A real home, with two cats, a small garden and even a picket fence.

He'd bought this house for her as soon as he was out of med school and had a salary that could stretch to mortgage payments on top of the rent for his studio loft apartment, and one of the saddest things about the aftermath of Sharon Cooper's stroke in her early fifties had been the fear that she was going to lose the dream of living in her perfect home.

At least he'd been able to do something about that. He'd promised that he would do everything he possibly could to make sure she never had to leave this house. He visited several times a week to take care of things like mowing the lawns or changing a light-bulb and he covered the cost of a home help that came daily to do any housework or meal preparation that his mother hadn't been able to manage.

'You hungry, Mum?' he called. 'I've made your favourite. Shepherd's pie.'

'Starving,' Sharon Cooper called back. 'It smells so good.'

She appeared in the kitchen doorway as she spoke, stopping for a moment to catch the doorframe with her strong hand. Trying hard to disguise her limp. Automatically, Blake reached out to offer her support but she brushed his hand away.

'I can manage. I'm doing better. The physiotherapist says I'm still making really good progress. I'll be back to normal one of these days.'

'You will be. I'm proud of you.' As he

spooned servings of the meal onto plates, Blake kept a corner of his eye on his mother's movements as she pulled out a chair and sat down at the tiny table by the window. He *was* proud of her. She'd fought for every inch of her recovery so far and she wasn't showing any signs of giving up before she reached her goal.

And why would she? She'd had to fight for everything in her life from her early years as a foster kid to being a single mother as a young adult, never earning enough to make life any easier. It was heartbreaking that she had had to face yet another huge challenge in this part of her life.

He set the plates on the table and then sat opposite his mother, putting a smile on his face.

'I've made enough to feed an army. You can freeze it when it cools down.'

'I might just eat it every night. It's delicious.' But Sharon's glance was stern. 'You don't need to do this all the time, you know. You've got enough to be doing without fussing about me.'

'You spent a fair few years looking after me, Mum. It's the least I can do.'

'Hmm. I'm sure you've got better things to be doing than making shepherd's pie. When do you get time to do fun stuff?'

'I do plenty of fun stuff.'

'Like helping out at that clinic like you did last night? It's just more work.'

'I like doing it.'

Not strictly true, he had to admit. It was often difficult to keep up his commitment to working two or three evenings a month and sometimes, it was a challenge that left him drained. The free clinic had its share of people embittered by poverty who could become pretty abusive but he also saw people who were grateful for any help and, along with his SDR work, it was another kind of freedom. You could save lives there, too. Like diagnosing a baby with meningitis when there was still time to treat them and an overwhelmed young mother might have put off seeking help that would have cost too much that week.

'And I think it's an important thing to do.'

His mother's gaze had softened.

'It is. I wish there'd been one when you were little. I felt so guilty that time that your eardrum burst when I didn't take you to the doctor in time for your earache just because I was hoping you'd be okay till payday.'

And if his mother had had a free clinic available back then, she might have had her high blood pressure diagnosed and treated before it had caused the damage that had led to her stroke.

'It didn't do me any harm.' He grinned as he reached for his phone as a text message pinged. 'See? I can hear perfectly well.'

'Who's texting you? A girl, I hope.'

'No. I'm not seeing anyone at the moment.' He read the message, frowned for a moment and then tapped in a rapid response.

'What happened to…oh, no… I've forgotten her name. They never last long enough for it to sink in and you never bring them to meet me.'

Blake grinned again. 'I've forgotten too.' He picked up his fork. Of course he never brought them to meet his mother. That was a step along the road to commitment. To having someone dependent on him and a mortgage on a house in the suburbs somewhere.

'That was a request for me to take an introductory USAR course up in Brisbane next weekend. The guy who was taking it came off his mountain bike and will be out of action for a while and they don't have anyone available locally.'

'Are you going to do it?'

'No reason not to. They pay for the flights and a hotel.'

Training weekends were a bit of a bonus. Easy extra money that could go straight into the account that covered Sharon's needs.

'It's lucky I've got a free weekend for once. And who knows? I might need a favour like this myself one day. Don't worry, I'll drop in before I go and make sure you've got everything you need.'

'I'll be fine. You go and have fun.' She looked up from her meal a minute later. 'You haven't had a callout for a while, have you? Not since that bush fire.' Sharon shook her head. 'Terrible business, that was. I don't know how you do it, love, but I'm very proud that you're one of the people who can. Where would we be without people like your team in the SD... P?'

'SDR, Mum. Specialist Disaster Response.'

'Oh, that's right. I thought it might be P for People.'

They ate in silence for a minute or two.

The acronym echoed in Blake's head. In Samantha Braithwaite's voice.

'I'd really like the opportunity to join the SDR team.'

What did she think it was all about? A bit of excitement to break the confines of working in a nice, controlled environment?

It was so much more than that to Blake. A window into the kind of world he'd hankered after when he'd set his sights on joining MSF. A world where you had to rely on every ounce of courage and skill you had and then some, sometimes.

It was freedom, that's what it was. The kind of freedom he'd been chasing his whole life.

People like Sam wouldn't get that. She came from a world full of comforts and the kind of freedom that money could always buy. Full of opportunity to do exactly what she wanted to do and the time and money to do frivolous things that would never have crossed his mother's mind.

'Do you ever get manicures, Mum?'

Sharon laughed. 'That's an odd question. Why would I pay someone else to do something I can do myself?' Then her smile faded.

'Not that I can manage it so well these days. I get Margo to cut my nails when they need it.'

'Would you like to go to a salon? Get a pretty colour or something? Did you know that you can get things like polka dots on your nails now?'

His mother was smiling again. 'I've seen that in the magazines. Nail art, they call it. Ridiculous.'

'Mmm.' About as ridiculous as the idea of having Sam join the SDR team.

'But a pretty colour isn't a bad idea. I'll put some polish on my shopping list and Margo can help me.'

'Just clear, thanks.'

'What, *no* colour?' The young manicurist looked shocked.

'It really isn't appropriate for where I work,' Sam said quietly. 'I really shouldn't have let you talk me into those dots last time.'

'She's a nurse,' the older woman in the next chair said. 'In the emergency department, did I tell you that?'

The manicurist smiled. 'Yes, you did, Mrs Braithwaite. You must be very proud of her.'

'Oh, I am… Sam, darling, why don't you

get a very pale pink? It will still look perfectly natural. You can always go a bit wild with your toes.'

'Sure.' Sam closed her eyes. A muscle in her jaw began to ache as she forced herself to keep her hands very still.

She was so over this spa business but it had become such a thing in her mother's life.

'It's the only way we get to spend some real time together—just you and me, darling. You have to sit still for an hour and there's nothing to do but talk...'

At least she'd escaped from a weekly ritual, pleading uncooperative shift hours or other commitments. These days, it was more likely to only be once a month but, if anything, it had made the sessions more precious to Sarah Braithwaite and breaking free of the constraints of being the 'perfect' daughter was proving to be almost impossible.

And increasingly frustrating.

What had seemed like a huge step forward, in moving into her own apartment a few years ago wasn't enough.

She loved her job but it wasn't quite enough, either. Not now that she was within touching distance of something like the SDR team that could offer so much more.

Sam had her hands under the drier now and her mother was having her nails painted. Bored, she let her gaze drift up to the walls of the salon where it snagged on a picture of a peaceful scene with horses grazing in a mountain meadow. Sarah followed her gaze.

'That grey one looks just like Trinity.'

'Mmm.' A wave of something like grief caught Sam's breath. 'I still miss her.'

'Maybe you should have kept her, darling. Just for trekking or something.'

'She loved eventing, Mum. And she was a champion. It wouldn't have been fair to keep her when I stopped competing.'

It had seemed a no-brainer at the time, to give up her beloved sport. In the months following her brother's death, she had lost any interest in what had been a teenage passion. It wasn't just that she knew how much her parents had always worried about the risk of injury. Sam realised now that part of her lifestyle changes had been due to the notion that she didn't deserve to be having fun. Not when her family was so utterly miserable and her beloved brother could never have any fun again.

'But you might be right. I could start riding again. It would be good exercise.'

'As long as you don't go back to jumping. That's *so* dangerous.'

This time it was a wave of what felt like weariness that washed over Sam. She closed her eyes, mentally hanging onto the bars of an emotional prison. One that she had, albeit, stepped into willingly enough when she was eighteen. When her parents' precious firstborn and only son had been so tragically killed. The one that enforced the rule that she was responsible for protecting the people she loved. That she had to protect herself in order to protect them. More than once, she had wondered if her failure to commit to any long-term relationship was, at some level, an unwillingness to strengthen the walls of that prison. To add someone else to the group of people she had to protect.

Her breath escaped in a small sigh. 'Life's dangerous, Mum. You can get killed crossing a road, you know.'

The silence that followed her comment was long enough to make her open her eyes again.

A sideways glance showed that her mother was blinking rapidly.

'Sorry… I'm not trying to stir up painful memories. I miss Alistair too. Every day.'

Sarah sniffed and pasted a bright smile on her face. 'You were both such little daredevils. As bad as each other. You with your horses and Al with his mountains.'

Sam reached out to touch her mother's arm. 'You let us follow our hearts and our passions and be who we wanted to be. You can't ask more of a parent than that.'

'Aww…' The manicurist looked up from her task. 'What a lovely thing to say.'

'But…' Sarah was biting her lip. 'You gave up *your* passion.'

'It wasn't fun any more. But…one day, I might want to do something else that has its own risks. I can't promise that I won't do that, if it's something I feel passionate enough about.'

'I wouldn't want you to, darling. If there's one thing that always gives me comfort, it's that Al died doing the one thing he loved more than anything else. He died instantly in that rock fall so I tell myself he wouldn't have known anything about it. He would have died happy.'

'I tell myself the same thing.' Sam's vision blurred a little with unshed tears.

'And that's all I want for you, too,' Sarah whispered. 'To do what makes you happy. I'll always worry about you but that's just part of the job description of being a mother. And I know you're too sensible to do something *really* dangerous.'

Maybe now wasn't the best time to tell her mother about the new passion that was too compelling to resist. Or the online bookings she had finalised last night.

One step at a time.

This had been a bit of a breakthrough, though. Sam could almost see a shiny key in the doorway of that self-imposed prison. Another step or two and the iron bars of that door could very well swing open.

'I almost forgot,' she said casually. 'I'm away next weekend at a training course. Friday evening to Sunday.'

'Oh? Like that resuscitation course you went to last year?'

'Something like that. A bit more specialised, even.'

Sarah smiled, including the manicurist in the conversation. 'That's my girl. Always having to learn something new and get even better at her job.'

'Good for you.' The young woman didn't look up from the attention she was giving Sarah's final nail. 'I love getting away for a weekend. Hope it's somewhere nice.'

'Should be,' Sam murmured. 'It's in Brisbane.'

CHAPTER FOUR

Nooo...

Sam's heart sank so hard it took her body along with it. She was actually slithering lower on this hard, plastic chair towards the back of a classroom located at a Brisbane emergency response centre that housed both fire service and ambulance vehicles and personnel.

This couldn't be happening.

She'd double checked. Harriet's casual comment that Blake Cooper was involved with USAR training had been a flashing warning sign when she'd booked herself into this introductory course and she'd gone back to check the trainer's name again before she filled in her registration details. It had been Adam Smith. A reassuringly ordinary name. A complete stranger.

Did Blake have an identical twin brother who'd been adopted out at birth and had a different name?

One that wore faded jeans and cowboy boots and had his hair tied back in a casual ponytail?

He hadn't spotted her yet, amongst the dozen or so people settling in here, so maybe she could quietly sneak out while he was busy slotting that memory stick into the computer linked to a data projector. Even as the cowardly thought slipped past, an image filled a large portion of the whiteboard at the front of the room and Sam was transfixed. People around her stopped arranging their notepads and water bottles and the murmur of conversation faded away. They were all staring.

The background of the image were buildings that had been destroyed by an earthquake or explosion, perhaps, and were now a mountain of rubble. Rescuers wearing hard hats and bright vests were dotted over the rubble and in the foreground was a team of people carrying a stretcher. Their faces were streaked with grime and their expressions conveyed a mixture of weariness, determination and satisfaction. In the midst of the horrific destruction, they had found someone alive.

Letters appeared slowly, one by one on the bottom of the image. U. S. A. R. And then words followed rapidly enough to create a sense of urgency. Urban Search and Rescue.

Sam felt herself straightening in her chair.

She was going to be one of those people in a hard hat and high-vis vest. Searching through rubble and triumphantly carrying a survivor away from an unthinkable disaster.

She wasn't going to be intimidated by anyone.

'Morning, all.'

The easy grin from their instructor unexpectedly caught Sam's attention with just as much of an impact as the image had. She hadn't seen him really smile before, she realised. And, man…it was some smile. Confident. Almost…cheeky?

It advertised charm. No, more than that. It was just confirming something she already knew.

Blake Cooper had charisma.

And, in the space of two words and a smile, he had the total attention of every person in this room.

'My name's Blake,' he told them. 'I'm an emergency doctor from Sydney but I've been involved with USAR for some years now. My mate, Adam, was supposed to be taking this course but he had a little mishap with his mountain bike and he's off work for a few days with a dislocated shoulder. You'll have to put up with me, I'm afraid.'

The ripple of laughter, notably from a woman in the front row, suggested that it wouldn't be a hardship. Blake was still smiling as his gaze travelled over the rest of the room.

The moment he spotted Sam was the moment the smile vanished. He actually froze for a moment as he caught her gaze and the intensity of that eye contact made her forget how to breathe.

Okay…maybe she was a *little* intimidated.

She wasn't going to break the eye contact, however. It was Blake who looked away to continue scanning the rest of his audience. It had taken all of a split second. Had she imagined that he'd almost jerked his head to do so?

No. Someone in front of her turned his head to give her a curious glance as Blake started speaking again. A 'what's so special about you?' kind of glance.

'Welcome,' Blake was saying. 'It's great to see so many people interested in finding out what USAR is all about. You won't get to the end of this weekend as qualified USAR technicians but you will get a certificate of attendance and you'll know whether it's something you'd like to get more involved with. And you will be in a position to be a valuable first responder if you're ever unlucky enough to find yourself in a disaster situation. As an ice-breaker, let's go around the room and find out what it is that's persuaded you to give up a weekend to do this course.'

Sam was in a bit of a disaster situation right now. What was she going to say when it got to her turn? Something along the lines of 'there's this guy who thinks he's going to stop me doing what I want and I'm here to prove he's wrong'?

The woman in the front row, who'd laughed so appreciatively at the idea of having to 'put up' with Blake as an instructor was apparently a paramedic, called Andrea, who wanted to increase her skill set.

There were several people who volunteered

with the Red Cross and had decided to do this course together.

The young man who'd turned to look at her, Wayne, and his friend beside him, Sean, were both members of a volunteer, rural fire-fighting team.

'We both want to get into the fire service for real,' Wayne said, 'and doing this course is a prerequisite for starting the unit stan-dards that we'll be doing if we get accepted. We thought it would be a good head start.'

'Good thinking.' Blake nodded. 'The com-petition to get into training programmes like the fire service or ambulance is getting tougher every year. Doing things like this, off your own bat, will definitely give you an extra tick on the check list for suitability.'

His words stayed with Sam as she listened to more people introduce themselves. By the time he nodded at her, she'd come up with something to say.

'Hi. I'm Sam Braithwaite. I'm an emer-gency department nurse from Sydney. I've already done a lot of postgraduate studies in things like trauma management and resusci-tation, and I want to be able to use my skills in a wider field.'

Blake's smile was tight. 'You've come a long way to do this course, Sam. I hope it lives up to your expectations.'

He was turning away and picking up his laser pointer, clearly intending to get straight into the course overview but Sam hadn't quite finished what she wanted to say.

'I liked what you said—about doing a course like this being helpful when it comes to getting chosen for something you really want to be a part of.' She smiled as she heard the murmur of agreement from the two young men in front of her. 'I'm sure we're all hoping you're right.'

'Mmm.' The sound Blake managed to make in response was merely a polite acknowledgment.

Samantha Braithwaite was here for only one reason that he could think of—to use the course as a stepping stone in her efforts to join the SDR team at Bondi Bayside.

He had to respect her determination and the ability to have identified something that would be a real bonus on her CV as far as the SDR criteria was concerned.

He also had to acknowledge that she couldn't have known he'd be taking the course.

This was karma. Fate had deemed that he needed punishment for the way he'd responded when she'd asked him about joining the team. There was nothing he could do about this situation but it was…annoying. He'd expected a relaxing weekend doing something easy and suddenly it had become complicated. That smile on her face right now told him just how complicated it was going to be because he was instantly distracted. It was a hopeful smile, accompanied by what looked like a plea from those huge, blue eyes.

He had the power to give her something she clearly wanted very badly.

Looking like that, he was sure that most men would cave instantly. But he wasn't most men. He turned away, clicking the laser pointer. Part of his brain registered relief that she'd toned down her clothing today, mind you. There were no long, brown legs on display or a frilly, feminine shirt. He'd noticed the practical cargo pants and a plain, loose T-shirt. Her hair wasn't flowing everywhere, either. It lay in a single plait over her shoulder.

She was still a princess, though. Just in disguise.

'There are a lot of other factors, of course,' he added, as he clicked the button. 'But it's certainly a good start.'

A new image filled the screen now and lines of text appeared as Blake began to explain what this two-day course was going to cover.

'USAR is a specialised technical rescue capability,' he told them. 'It's designed for the location and rescue of entrapped people following some kind of structural collapse. Anyone got any ideas what could cause structural collapse?'

'Earthquakes,' Andrea offered. 'You see USAR teams on the news all the time, getting deployed to big earthquakes.'

She was smiling at him as she spoke and it was impossible to miss the admiration in her eyes. An invitation, even, that he might have found interesting under normal circumstances but not today. It wasn't remotely appealing when Sam was in the same room and that was annoying, as well. Maybe that was why he smiled back, as he nodded and turned towards Wayne, who'd raised his hand.

'Floods,' Wayne said. 'We get a lot of those in this part of the country. A decent flood will destroy a lot of buildings.'

'And cyclones.' Sean nodded. 'They often go together.'

'Landslides,' someone else said.

'Explosions?' An older man, Tom, who had a background in Civil Defence, sounded tentative but Blake nodded encouragingly.

'You're right. It could be from an industrial accident or, these days unfortunately, it could be due to a terrorist attack. It's certainly up there on the list of possibilities. Anything else?'

There was a moment's thoughtful silence and despite himself, Blake's gaze settled on Sam, who hadn't contributed.

'Fire?'

Sean gave Wayne a light punch on his arm. 'We should have thought of that one,' he whispered loudly.

Sam blinked. 'Oh…would that be the responsibility of the fire service rather than a specialised rescue team?'

'If it involves structural collapse then, yes, USAR could be involved alongside the fire service,' Blake said. 'It could be in a high-rise building, perhaps. Or secondary to an earthquake. Or a bush fire that involves dwellings. In fact, that was the last deployment I went on, although that was with a specialist disaster response team rather than a purely USAR unit. Anyway…now that we've got a scope of the type of disasters we could be dealing with, let's have a look at our programme and see what we'll be covering.'

He put the timetable up on the screen. He'd be taking them through how a scene size-up was done and how to look for potential voids that could indicate the potential for survivors. He'd do a session on structural hazards and hazard mitigation procedures and then they could move onto location techniques and rescue, including shoring for the stabilisation of damaged structures.

'We'll cover some basic first aid,' he finished up, 'although that's obviously going to be redundant for some of you.' He glanced at Andrea, the paramedic, and then towards Sam. 'Maybe you guys can help me teach that session.'

'Sure,' Andrea said. 'I'd be delighted.'

'The grand finale will be an opportunity to take part in a training exercise. Members of the USAR team in Brisbane—a lot of whom are firies and paramedics who are working at this base—will be preparing a scene for us at a building supplies dumping ground just out of town. You'll get to do a line and hail search and a rescue, if you can find anyone alive.'

An excited murmur ran around the room but Blake raised his hand. 'There's a lot to get through first,' he warned. 'And a test at the end of our classroom time. I won't be letting anyone on site if I'm not confident that you can keep yourself safe. And I should warn you that it's going to be physically challenging. And probably dirty.'

His gaze skated past one of the older women from the Red Cross group who was looking worried to the back of the room.

He was expecting Sam to be looking just as disconcerted by the prospect of something physically demanding but he couldn't have been more wrong. The excitement level in the room might have faded somewhat with his warning but it hadn't left Sam's face.

Glowing…that was the only word for it.

If he hadn't realised just how passionate she was about this, he certainly did now. But it puzzled him.

Why was this *so* important to her?

Maybe it was him who was feeling disconcerted. Why did it suddenly seem so important that he find the answer to that question?

Because he couldn't figure out why a princess would actually want to get down and dirty with rescue work?

Because the idea was kind of...*hot*?

Oh, man...this weekend was going to test his strength of character for resisting temptation big time.

'Let's get into it.' He needed to focus. He picked up a stack of workbooks and began distributing them. 'We'll start at the beginning and look at how we size up a scene. You'll find all the information you'll need in these books and there's plenty of space to make your own notes.'

Sam was getting writer's cramp well before they had their first, proper break at lunchtime. She intended to memorise everything to ensure that she got a hundred per cent on the test they would be having tomorrow.

Maybe it was actually a good thing that Blake Cooper had unexpectedly ended up being her tutor here. She had two whole days to make sure he knew exactly how committed she was to being part of the SDR. She just had to make sure he also discovered how competent she could be.

She was learning a lot. Viable voids were spaces where surviving victims could be located and rescued from. Structural hazards included falling loose debris, shifting of a debris pile or the dropping of higher components like when a damaged wall buckled under the weight of a roof. Risk management meant staying away from dangerous areas if there was no good reason to be there and limiting the number of people going into a hazardous area or the time they spent in there. Hazards could be reduced by removing debris, using monitors to detect building movement or stabilisation, which was costly in terms of time and resources but necessary in high risk areas when the possibility of extricating victims was also high.

Sam listened avidly, studied diagrams and images, joined in the discussions and wrote endless extra notes. She was totally focused on her learning but that didn't stop her awareness of their tutor growing with every passing minute and then hour.

It was his quick thinking at first. The way Blake could instantly catch the thread of what someone was trying to say. And his teaching ability—the way he could ask leading questions that led his students to really think about something and understand the theory behind the knowledge.

And then it was the sound of his voice. The casual confidence in the way he spoke and tones that ranged from an amusement bordering on laughter, a sharpness that advertised a keen intelligence to what she could only think of as a deep—and sexy—rumble.

By that afternoon, Sam was acutely aware of every movement of his body as well. He used his hands often when he was describing something and her gaze instantly locked on them at the slightest flicker even as she focused on what he was saying.

Big, strong hands. No jewellery, apart from a heavy-looking watch, although those long fingers could have pulled off a ring and still looked completely masculine, and a leather wristband or something would have looked cool and fitted that maverick, cowboy type of vibe.

There was a point, when Blake was explaining the difference between raker shores used to stabilise the outside of a structure and the vertical shores that were then used to create a safer passage internally, when Sam's concentration wavered.

Something twisted deep in her belly as she stared at his hands and her brain just had to go and imagine what it would feel like if those hands were touching her body. And then the twist blossomed into such a kick of the most delicious—and, okay—irresistible desire, that she had to close her eyes just for a second.

How on earth had he noticed that?

'Sam—you want to tell us the difference between a T shore and a double T shore?'

'Ah…'

Had he *guessed* what she'd been thinking?

Good grief…how mortifying would that be? It would hand him confirmation of what he thought about her, wouldn't it? That she was some kind of blonde bimbo who had no right being here, let alone joining his SDR team.

Fortunately, her brain hadn't been completely on strike. A lightning-fast glance at her notes and she had her response.

'A T shore is quick to put up but is only marginally stable. A double T that uses two vertical four-by-four posts plated to the top horizontal one is the most stable spot support.'

'Hmm...' He held her gaze for a heartbeat longer. 'Good.'

Was she imagining a hint of disappointment? Or was it puzzlement? She hadn't quite figured out what it meant when Blake rubbed the back of his neck like that. She was, unconsciously, building a library of his body movements, though. She could see the way he hitched one hip onto the edge of a desk when he was settling in to make sure his students understood exactly what he was trying to teach. Did he realise how he could encourage people to get to the right answer by the way he moved his eyebrows? And as for the way the tip of tongue appeared to dampen his lips when his enthusiasm was sparked by listening to a question...

Phew...

By the time the intensive, theoretical day had ended, Sam was a curious mix of being both tired and wired. And the buzz wasn't just from all the fascinating information she had absorbed. No. Sam knew perfectly well that the escalating attraction to Blake Cooper had to be responsible for a large part of that buzz.

Lunch had been provided during course time but dinner wasn't. Wayne suggested that the class go to a pizza restaurant within easy walking distance and there was widespread enthusiasm from all the participants that didn't have to get back to family commitments.

'Blake?' he asked. 'You wanna come and have some pizza and a beer with us?'

Sam deliberately didn't look up as she stuffed her workbook and pens into her shoulder bag.

She wanted him to come because that would mean more time being aware of that attraction and…and how alive it made her feel.

But she didn't want him to come because she'd have to be on guard all the time and make sure she didn't say something stupid or…or drop a slice of pizza or something.

She wanted him to come because it would be the first time she'd seen him in a social setting and, while she didn't think it would

make him behave any differently, she was
curious to find out.

She didn't want him to come because it
would mean that the safety barriers of having a professional reason to be in his company would be less visible and...and *anything*
could happen.

Okay. Wanting him to come had just re-
soundingly won the internal battle and, at the
same moment, she heard Blake speak.

'Sure...why not? I need to have a chat
with some of the guys on station here first,
to make sure we're set up for tomorrow, but
I'll join you soon.'

Several wood-fired, delicious-smelling piz-
zas had been delivered to the long, wooden
table before Blake joined the group but, for
a long time, Sam found it easy to resist the
temptation. She was too distracted by keeping a corner of her eye on the doorway that
led out to this garden, waiting for a glimpse
of those cowboy boots or the shape of that
long, lean body heading towards her. Would
he have taken his ponytail down so that he
looked like a guitarist from some cool rock
band again? Like he had the first time she'd

seen him in the ED, when she'd made the incorrect assumption that he was the baby's father and not a doctor?

The conversation around her was lively.

'I can't wait for tomorrow,' Wayne said. 'I'm not so keen on all this theoretical stuff. I want to learn about the search techniques. Be out there throwing some rubble around and actually rescuing someone.'

'Yeah…' Sean was nodding. 'What's a "line and hail" search, d'ya reckon? What's the weather got to do with it?'

Everybody laughed and Tom smiled. 'Hail isn't just icy rain, Sean. It's another word for calling out to somebody.'

Wayne shook his head. 'You're an idiot, mate.'

'Hey…and you think you can just *throw* rubble around? You wanna give yourself someone else that needs rescuing?'

But the friends were grinning at each other. And then Sean pushed a platter closer to Sam.

'You not eating? This one's really good. Meat lovers.'

'This one's better…' Andrea held out another platter. 'Vegetarian with extra cheese.'

'Mmm…' Sam took a wedge of the vegetarian pizza and then took a big bite. There was definitely extra cheese. A long string of mozzarella was still attached to the rest of the slice as she pulled it away from her mouth. She lifted her hand up high enough to break the string, which then fell into a coil all over her face. With one hand still holding her pizza and the other trying to pull cheese off her face, it was the worst possible moment to notice that Blake had finally arrived. That Wayne and Sean were moving to make space for him, in fact. Directly opposite her.

He had a frosty bottle of lager in his hand, with a wedge of lime stuffed into the neck, a one-sided smile and a gaze that was firmly fixed on Sam's face.

'Looks like you're getting into it,' he said.

'Mmm…'

With a wave of something like relief, Sam realised she might as well give up worrying about her image in front of this man. She was doomed. And, with that realisation, she relaxed, smiled back at him and broke one of her mother's sternest childhood rules of not speaking with your mouth full.

'It'sh great. Try shome…'

Even Blake looked surprised at her rule

breaking. His smile widened to include both sides of his mouth.

'I think I will. That looks like it's got jalapenos on it.' He reached for a huge triangle, expertly dealing with the string of cheese that trailed after it. 'My favourite.'

He took a huge bite and Sam couldn't look away. Wasn't that another note in her mother's etiquette bible—that it was rude to watch people eat?

Why was it that every movement he made was so fascinating?

Clearly Andrea was sharing the fascination. She even leaned further across the table towards Blake.

'I've been dying to ask you,' she said. 'What's the most exciting thing you've ever done, Blake?'

Blake stopped chewing.

The answer to that question that popped—uninvited—straight into his head was that the most exciting thing he'd ever done was quite possibly 'sitting across the table, right now, from Samantha Braithwaite'.

That jolt of sensation when he'd caught sight of her pulling that string of cheese off her face and then making it disappear between her parted lips hadn't worn off yet, despite trying to distract himself with food.

He'd been doing so well, today, too.

He'd been so aware of her in his classroom. He'd actually been able to *feel* her gaze on his skin whenever he was talking and it had been a conscious effort not to let his own line of sight connect with hers any more often than would have been normal, but he'd never been more aware of what was in his peripheral vision.

He now knew how straight Sam sat when she was listening to something that interested her and that she was inclined to fiddle with something at the same time, like her pen or the end of that long braid hanging over her shoulder. He had learned the timbre of her voice and it had the same effect as hearing a favourite song on the radio when he walked into a café. He just wanted to stand still for a moment and listen. To turn up the volume...

He knew that Sam had the bluest eyes of anyone he'd ever met. Did she wear contacts to get that extraordinary depth of colour?

It hadn't made any significant difference that she was wearing those practical, loose-fitting clothes today. His memory banks had been only too happy to use a kind of mental photo-editing software and superimpose a pair of faded denim shorts over those cargo pants and replace the T-shirt with a soft top that not only revealed a delicious cleavage but had the bonus of being just a little transparent.

And now, here they were in a social situation. With food and alcohol and loud music coming from within the trendy restaurant. A drum beat that was an invitation to break rules and get a little wild.

Oh, yeah…it was exciting, all right.

A damn shame it wouldn't be going any further but it wasn't exactly unpleasant. A bit like holding an expensive gift he had no intention of unwrapping but it was irresistible to pick it up and feel its shape and wonder what might be hidden inside. Not that he was doing that on a conscious level, of course. He hadn't bothered trying to analyse how it was making him feel at all, until Andrea had asked that question.

The shock of realising just how much being this close to Sam was affecting him must have been evident in some facial twitch because Andrea grimaced, apologetically.

'I mean…you know…with USAR?'

'Ah…' Blake finally swallowed his mouthful of pizza as he nodded and then gave Andrea his laziest smile. 'In that case, I guess it's okay to tell you.'

'And how often do you get called out?' Wayne asked. 'For real, I mean?'

'I'm not involved with a dedicated USAR team right now,' Blake said. 'I'm part of a specialised disaster response team at my hospital and we can be called out to almost anything—from a multi-car pile-up to a cyclone at the other end of the country—so we actually get called out a lot. We're a medical response, but we have team members like myself who have USAR qualifications and we work closely with other teams who can already be on scene.'

He risked a quick glance across the table as he took another bite of his pizza. Sam wasn't looking at him but she wasn't eating, either. She was breaking little pieces of her pizza crust off. Fiddling.

She was listening…

'Before we set up our hospital-based team,

I used to belong to a USAR unit. A few years ago we responded to a big earthquake in China. There were teams there from all over the world and we were on site for nearly two weeks. I reckon the most exciting thing was finding someone alive who'd been trapped for ten days. I'll never forget hearing the sound of his voice on that line and hail search.'

His peripheral vision told him that Sam's fingers had stilled. And he could feel that gaze on his skin again, as if the hairs on his arm had lifted slightly.

'Talk us through that,' Wayne said eagerly. 'How does it work?'

'The team is in a line, obviously.' Blake smiled. 'And you get assigned an area to cover. There's a safety officer whose job it is to identify and mark hazards and you take turns calling along the line and then stay quiet to see if anybody can hear anything. You'll learn all about this in the morning.'

But everyone around the table stayed quiet. They wanted to hear more now.

'What do you call?' Sean asked. 'Is it like "Can anyone hear me?"'

'Pretty much. Usually, it's "Rescue team above, can you hear me?" Or, sometimes, if there's a bit of metal poking through the rubble, like some reinforcing poles, you can tap on it with a rock or something. Sounds like that can travel a lot further than a human voice.'

'And they tap back? Is that how you found that guy still alive?'

'Actually, I heard his voice. Very faintly. I was on the end of that line and we'd been searching all day and it was the last thing I expected to hear. Nobody had been found alive for the last five days.'

'So what happened then, after you heard him?'

It was the first contribution Sam had made to this conversation and it would have been rude not to look at her but, when he did, his response seemed to vanish and it felt like he was simply staring.

It was only for the space of a heartbeat but he knew that Sam was aware of that tiny pause just as much as he was.

Tom saved it becoming awkward. 'Did you start digging straight away?'

'No. There's a protocol. You have to pinpoint, as best you can, exactly where the sound is coming from. That means changing the position of everybody in the line to try and surround where you think it's coming from. And then you have to plan how to remove the debris and start well away from where the victim is because you don't know what position they're lying in or how stable the void is.'

'That must have been *so* exciting,' Andrea said. 'To get him out…'

'It was,' Blake admitted. 'But I think the biggest thrill was to hear that response in the first place.' He took a long pull of his lager. 'It's weird because you're part of a team but it can feel like you're working alone at the same time.'

Why was he telling them this stuff? He wasn't into discussing feelings.

Maybe it was because he could still feel that prickle on his skin that told him how intently Sam was listening to every word he said.

For some weird reason, he didn't want to stop.

'It's kind of like being lost and walking for the longest time and then seeing a tiny star of light up ahead that tells you that maybe you're not going to be alone for much longer.' He pulled a self-deprecating face. 'It's hard to describe but maybe some of you will actually get to experience it one day.'

Blake helped himself to another piece of pizza. 'Enough shop talk,' he said. 'And eat up, guys. You're going to need plenty of energy tomorrow.'

Wow...

Sam excused herself to go to the restroom a short time later and ended up splashing a bit of cold water on her face.

Who knew that Blake Cooper had a poetic streak? The image he had conjured up was still haunting her—of him lost and alone in some wilderness, pushing himself towards a goal of...what...being rescued or *not* being alone? Or maybe they were the same thing.

He could be in a team and still feel alone?

That broke her heart but she could understand it.

Sometimes Sam felt lonely in the middle of a crowd. And sometimes she was afraid she would feel like that for the rest of her life. Because she was scared to let people close enough that she wouldn't feel alone? Because, even though it was suffocating to be wrapped in cotton wool, it was too scary to imagine existing without it?

Maybe the scariest thing had been that urge to reach across the table when Blake had been speaking.

To take hold of his hand, tightly enough to let him know that he didn't need to feel alone any more.

She knew it would be a bad idea to go and sit back at that table opposite Blake but her feet still took her in that direction. Was it disappointment or relief that washed over her when she saw that he'd already gone?

'I'm going to head back to my hotel,' she told the others. 'I'll see you all tomorrow.'

Pushing through the crowd near the bar, Sam didn't see the man whose arm brushed hers.

But she knew who it was instantly.

'I thought you'd gone,' she said in surprise.

'Only to get another beer. But I'll be heading home soon. Where are you going?'

'Back to my hotel.' She wasn't about to admit to her tutor that she needed some study time to make sure she aced the test tomorrow but sadly, her brain had to find a substitute reason. 'I need my beauty sleep,' she said.

The look Blake gave her was unreadable. Intense.

They were in the middle of a small, noisy crowd but it suddenly felt as if they were totally alone.

Together.

'I know what you meant,' Sam found herself saying softly. 'About being in a team but feeling like you're working alone.'

The intensity of that dark gaze increased. 'Oh? Do you really think that's the best thing to say to someone whose team you want to join?'

Oh, help…was she ruining any chance she might ever have to join the SDR?

'A team is made up of individuals,' she said carefully. 'Being aware of yourself doesn't mean you can't work with everybody else.'

Blake leaned closer as someone pushed past him. His head was much closer to hers now.

'And what are you aware of, Sam? When you're part of a team?'

'That people working together have a power you can never have alone. That that power can make it possible to get past the kind of boundaries that might otherwise hold you back.'

'And why do you want to get past those boundaries?'

'You have to,' she said quietly. 'If you ever want to find out who you really are and what you're capable of. Don't you think?'

The response was no more than a lifted eyebrow.

With a half-smile, Sam turned away and slipped through the crowd. She knew there were a lot of people between them by the time she got to the outside door of the restaurant.

But she also knew that Blake was still watching her.

CHAPTER FIVE

'OKAY... ARE WE READY? You all understand what you have to do?'

There was an enthusiastic, affirmative response from the line of people now standing in front of an impressive mound of hard waste. A lot of materials from demolished buildings got recycled but the rest of it ended up here, in a huge dump on the outskirts of Brisbane. Concrete blocks and bricks and lengths of curly, steel reinforcing rods, corrugated iron and wooden boards, broken doors, window frames and chimneys—even sections of carpeting and odds and ends of smashed furniture.

It was a dangerous environment that wasn't accessible to unauthorised people but parts of this dump were a perfect training ground for urban search and rescue personnel and they had used this particular section as an introductory exercise on many previous occasions.

The current course members were checking that they were the correct distance from each other. Dressed in the overalls and other safety gear provided, some were nervously adjusting items like their hard hats, knee pads, goggles or the dust masks covering mouths and noses. The person standing closest to Blake was holding an extra bit of gear—a can of fluorescent orange spray paint.

There'd been a few disappointed faces when he'd named Sam as the safety officer for this exercise because it was a key role that he would be working alongside. Yesterday morning, when he'd spotted her amongst his pupils, having her by his side like this would have been at the very top of any list of things he would never have considered. This afternoon, however, after an intensive theoretical session on line and hail searches followed by the test of what they'd taken on board so far, he hadn't hesitated for a moment in picking Sam.

It wasn't just that she'd scored a perfect hundred per cent on that test.

Or that he could sense she'd wanted this important role as much as, say, Wayne or Sean did.

No. It was all about what she'd said to him last night. Words that had echoed in his head long after she'd vanished back to wherever she was staying. Words—or maybe it was more like feelings—that had continued chasing him in his dreams.

She wanted to push herself. To find out who she really was and what she was capable of. Well...he could help with that right now. He was going to push her in this exercise.

Because maybe he wanted to find out who she really was and what she was capable of, too?

No, it was more than that. Her words had connected on a deeper level. He'd never tried analysing the effect that being a member of an elite team had had on him but it was true that he'd always pushed himself that bit harder when someone else was in the picture. A team member. Or a patient that needed help. Not that he'd seen boundaries. He'd just known that he had to try harder. Get better at what he needed to be able to do. Had he accomplished that because of the power she'd identified?

Sam also recognised that you could still feel alone amongst others. That battles were private as much as anything shared with even one other person, let alone a whole team.

And that made her different.

Intriguing.

So, yeah…he couldn't have picked anyone else from this group to work alongside him like this.

'You happy if we start?' he asked Sam.

'I can't see any obvious hazards for the first few steps. Oh, wait…what about that bent reinforcing rod there? And that corner of corrugated iron poking out?' The tin of paint rattled in her hand as she shook it. 'I'll mark them as hazards.'

A minute later and the line was waiting impatiently to take their first stride onto the rubbish pile. Blake raised his whistle to his lips and gave one long and one short blast as a signal to commence operations.

Wayne was the first person in the line.

'Rescue team above,' he yelled, when everybody moved forward a step. 'Can you hear me?'

Blake could sense everyone silently counting off ten seconds.

'Nothing heard,' Wayne reported.

Andrea was the last in the line. Had he
purposely put her as far away as possible?
She'd looked disappointed, too.

Her voice sounded quite faint. 'Rescue
team above, can you hear me?'

Blake directed the line to advance a stride
and scanned their movements. 'Three points
of contact with the debris at all times,' he
shouted. 'Don't forget. One foot, one hand,
then the other foot and the other hand. Look
out, Tom...'

Tom's hand had dislodged a brick that tum-
bled down to crash onto a sheet of corrugated
iron. Everyone froze and Blake's sideways
glance at Sam was a question.

'There's an overhang there that might have
been weakened by that brick getting dislodged,' she said.

'What are you going to do about it?'

'Mark it as a hazard?' Her gaze was steady.
'Or tell you so you can shift Tom to a safer
position?'

Before Blake could respond, there was a
sharp blast on a whistle.

'I can see something,' one of the Red Cross attendees called excitedly. 'I think it's a…it's a *foot*…'

'Okay.' Blake redeployed the line. 'Wayne, move forward a metre and then to your left a metre. Sean, come right and down a metre…' He soon had the group surrounding the point. 'Safety Officer—what do you think?'

'We need to move some of the larger pieces of debris. Like that door. And place it somewhere it's not going to cause a problem.'

Wayne and Sean lifted the door under Blake's direction and slid it sideways, uncovering more of the mannequin that had been 'buried'. As the medic for the team, Blake moved in and checked for a pulse.

'He's dead,' he announced. 'What now?'

'Sam's got the paint,' Sean responded. 'She marks it with a V for victim.'

Sam moved carefully, keeping her three points of contact, and sprayed the V on the surrounding debris. And then she remembered to put a line through the V denoting that this would be a body retrieval to be dealt with later, and not a live victim that the team could work to rescue.

She moved carefully back to her position

near Blake, keeping her points of contact and clearly testing each point for stability before trusting it with her body weight but he could sense the satisfaction this involvement had provided. When she glanced up, it was an automatic thing to do to nod and give her an approving smile.

This wasn't any kind of question for her to focus on and then respond to so it seemed to catch her off guard. Her eyes widened behind her goggles and held his for a heartbeat. And then another.

Okay, maybe there was a question there—on her part.

And, for the life of him, he had no defences to pull around him. He was the one who was off guard now.

He wanted this woman.

In his life.

In his bed…

Maybe Sam could see straight into his head through that eye contact. She certainly lost her focus for a moment and that made her scramble the order of her points of contact. With no grip for both hands, her foot slipped and she could have fallen onto something that might have hurt her if Blake hadn't reached out and caught her arm. He waited until she'd regained her balance and then he took her hand to help her step over an awkward pile of bricks.

They were both wearing gloves but he could have sworn he could feel the warmth of her skin against his.

And that should have been more than enough of a warning to step away.

The blast on his whistle felt like the first step in doing exactly that.

'Let's re-form the chain,' he called. 'And see if we can find a surviving victim this time.'

The afternoon wore on but there was no sign that the training session was going to be wrapped up anytime soon.

It was hot and Sam was aware of perspiration gluing the T-shirt she was wearing under these overalls to her skin. She could change her clothes before heading to the airport but how likely was it that she'd be able to find a shower? At least she'd chosen the latest flight available back to Sydney. Her plane didn't take off until ten p.m. tonight.

'Rescue team above…can you hear me?'

The call—and then the ten second silence

to listen for a response—was so familiar now it was almost boring.

'Nothing heard.'

'Rescue team above…can you hear me?'

Sam's mind wandered a little. She could imagine Blake doing this for real during that earthquake. Day after day of moving over vast piles of rubble, just a metre at a time. Hoping with each call that there would be a response and having that flicker of disappointment every time nothing was heard.

What did he think about when his mind wandered?

This morning, during that intensive theoretical session, she would have said that Blake wouldn't get distracted. That he was capable of a fierce concentration that nothing would dent.

But there'd been a moment a while back, when he'd grabbed her arm after that stupid slip and, even behind the screen of those plastic goggles, she'd seen something completely unexpected.

Something that was very personal. It had felt as if he was seeing her for the first time. *Really* seeing her.

And he liked what he saw…

Oh, man…

Focus, she ordered herself. *Ignore that totally inappropriate shaft of desire. One foot, one hand. Other foot…other hand.*

The single blast of a whistle at the other end of the line was so surprising it made her jump. Turning her head, she could see that Andrea had her arm raised—the signal that she'd heard something. The whistle blast had been to demand silence.

The call was repeated.

'Rescue team above…can you hear me?'

Andrea's arm shot up again. And so did Tom's.

Any hint of boredom after the last hour of slow movements and endlessly repeated calls evaporated instantly. It was ridiculous to feel this excited as Blake redeployed the line to large circle surrounding where the sound had been heard but it was easy to forget the reality that this was a staged exercise and imagine that it was for real.

That she was on the front line in an emergency situation, like an earthquake or a tsunami.

That she was working alongside Blake Cooper in the SDR.

And it was every bit as exciting as she'd known it would be.

It wasn't a voice that had been heard, it was a tapping sound. This time it was a live victim who was buried and they were responding to calls with what sounded like a rock hitting a metal pipe. Larger pieces of debris had to be moved and placed somewhere else under Sam's supervision as the safety officer. Smaller pieces were shifted into a pile that she used as a background to spray a V without a cross through it. This time they were actually rescuing somebody, not locating a dead body.

'I can see a void.' Tom sounded as excited as Sam was feeling. 'There's a window frame that's lying against an old sofa or something. There's definitely a triangle of space in there.'

'Talk to the victim,' Blake suggested. 'See if you can hear a voice now and not just the tapping.'

'Hey,' Tom called. 'Can you hear me?'

'Yes…' a male voice responded. 'Thank goodness. I've been waiting for ever to get rescued.'

'What's your name?'

'John.'

'Are you hurt, John?'

'My arm hurts.'

'Are you bleeding anywhere?' Wayne had moved closer to Tom and was trying to angle his headlamp into the void.

'Dunno…it's pretty dark in here. How 'bout getting me out, guys?'

'We're onto it, mate,' Wayne told him. 'Hang in there.'

Clearing more rubble to open the void had to be a careful process and Sam had to remind the other members of the team to slow down.

'We can't risk anything collapsing into the space where John is,' she said. 'One piece at a time and watch for any signs of movement in the debris pile around you.'

'The command station has been notified,' Blake told them as they worked. 'There are people bringing a Stokes basket and a first-aid kit to this location.'

It seemed to take a long time until the window frame could finally be tilted to reveal their victim. John was a young man, probably a volunteer from the fire crew based here. Sam looked at Blake, expecting him to examine John in his role as the team medic but, instead, he used this point in the exercise to reinforce earlier teaching.

'Apart from Andrea and Sam, who can tell me what you remember from our first-aid session? What are the three most important things?'

'ABC,' someone supplied. 'Airway, breathing and circulation.'

'What can we tell about John's airway?'

'He's talking,' Sean said. 'So his airway's open and he's able to breathe.'

'What can we do about circulation?'

'Check to see if there's any obvious bleeding,' Tom said. 'And if there is, we need to put pressure on the wound to stop it.'

'My arm hurts,' John said helpfully.

'If it's a fracture, we need to splint it,' one of the Red Cross volunteers offered. 'That will reduce the pain and the risk of further injuries when we move him.'

Blake nodded. 'Great. And how are we going to move him?'

'The Stokes basket has straps to secure the patient and handles on the sides for lifting and moving it.'

'How many people do we need?'

'Seven,' Sam said into the short silence

that followed as people tried to remember. This wasn't a question about basic first aid any more. 'Four people to lift the stretcher and two people standing in front. The front handles of the stretcher get passed to the two people in front and then the two people at the back move around them to stand in front.'

'That's only six people,' Blake pointed out. 'Who's the seventh?'

'The safety officer,' Wayne said. 'No, wait. It's the scout. He's checking to see the best way to go and whether it's safe.' He grinned at Sam. 'Or she.'

'Okay...' Blake was shielding his eyes from the glare of the sun that had dropped much lower in the sky. 'Great job, everyone. We'll call it a day, I think. It's getting late and I know that some of you have to travel to get home. Let's get down and we'll collect up all the gear.' He stretched out his hand to help John to his feet. 'Thanks for your help, mate.'

'Hey, no worries. It's my job to sort the gear and put it away when we get back, anyway.'

It was six p.m. by the time the bus took the group back to the fire station where they'd left their bags. Blake handed out the certificates of course completion to the group and had a few, final words to say.

'I hope this course will have inspired some of you to go further with USAR training,' he told them.

Wayne and Sean nodded enthusiastically. Sam felt herself drawing in a deeper breath. She wanted to nod as well. Instead, she just caught Blake's gaze as it travelled over the group with a steady, determined response. She wanted more than USAR training. She wanted to be part of the action of the SDR team.

'As I said at the start, this course is designed to give you the skills to be a first responder if you find yourselves in a disaster situation. Kind of like a public first aid course as opposed to becoming a doctor or a paramedic. You should, however, now be not only in a much better position to keep yourselves safe in a disaster, but you'll be an asset to the specialist personnel that will arrive as soon as possible. They'll be wanting any information you can give them on potential victims. And, if they know you've done this course, you could well be valuable extra team members. Good luck to you all and thanks for coming.'

People wanted to thank him as well but it was clear that everybody was keen to head home and probably straight into a shower. They were all tired and grubby after their hours at the dump. Sam could feel the grit in her hair and looked down at her stained T-shirt with dismay when the flurry of farewells had died down and the group had dispersed. She picked up her backpack and slung a strap over her shoulder. A glance behind her revealed Blake collecting training manuals and his USB stick. Another glance told her that she was the only pupil left now.

She hadn't thanked Blake yet but she wasn't quite sure what to say. He'd given her more than an insight into a world she wanted so much to be a part of.

He'd given her a glimpse of who he was, as well. Someone who walked alone even in the midst of a crowd.

What she felt about him had changed from being simply attraction.

It was more like a connection now. An understanding, anyway. She believed that Blake Cooper, on some level, lived with the same kind of loneliness that she did. That he had barriers as big as hers that made it impossible to connect with others in a way that made you—or them—too vulnerable.

'Still here?' Blake was moving towards the door. 'Are you staying on in Brisbane or heading back to Sydney tonight?'

'Heading back. I'm on an early shift to-morrow, in fact.'

'Me, too.' The glance in her direction held a note of respect and the tilt of his lips was a genuine smile. 'No rest for the wicked, huh?'

'Mmm.' Sam had to break the eye con-tact. Somehow, the word 'wicked' when she was standing so close to this man was a little overwhelming. With connotations that were a world away from the kind of activities they had been engaged in this weekend.

Blake held the door open for her and the courteous gesture felt like a gift.

'How are you getting to the airport?'

'I've called a taxi. I've got a bit of time, with my flight not leaving till ten p.m. I'm hoping I can find a shower and get to change my clothes. I'm filthy.'

Uh-oh… 'Filthy' also had connotations that had nothing to do with the dust and dirt she had gathered from head to toe.

Blake was silent as they walked to the

front of the building. The taxi was already there. Sam turned and opened her mouth to say goodbye and thank Blake but any words died on her lips. There was an odd look on his face that made her think he was struggling with something. That whatever he was about to say was…important?

'I'm going back on the same flight,' he said, 'and I got a late checkout at my hotel because I knew I'd need a shower.' He cleared his throat. 'Why don't we share your taxi and you could come back to my room and use my shower?'

Wow… This was totally unexpected. And… huge…

A gesture of friendship?

And then Sam remembered that look he'd given her when she'd slipped on the debris at the dump and he'd caught her arm to prevent her falling. When she'd had the impression he was really seeing her for the first time and that maybe he was impressed with what he could see.

Attracted, even…

Which made accepting this offer possibly not the wisest thing to do.

But it also made it irresistible.

Incredibly exciting, even…

'That would be awesome,' Sam heard herself saying. 'Infinitely better than an airport shower. Thanks, Blake.'

What *had* he been thinking?

He hadn't been able to stop himself making the offer because it would have been a perfectly normal thing to do with any of the team members he worked with on an exercise. And it *felt* like he'd been working with Sam as a team member out there on the dump.

She'd proved herself, hadn't she? She was smart and committed. And gutsy. Exactly the type of person that they would want to recruit to Bondi Bayside's SDR team. Maybe he'd even had the idea that he might have to rethink his aversion to her trying out for the team.

Except he'd known what kind of distraction she'd be, whether it was intended or not.

And, right now, he was being reminded in the strongest way possible precisely what kind of distraction that could be.

He could hear the water running in his bathroom behind the closed door.

He knew that Samantha Braithwaite was

standing in that glass cubicle. Naked. Maybe she was washing her hair and had bubbles flowing down the entire length of her body…

Oh, man… When it came to his turn, he'd need to turn the temperature control right down. A blast of icy cold water might do something towards getting his body under better control. Blake tightened the knot in the towel he'd wrapped around his waist after discarding his dirty clothes. He paced his room, keeping his gaze locked on the tablet he was holding. Maybe catching up on the latest MSF news would help.

It did.

Until the click of the bathroom door being opened made the words blur in front of his face.

A sideways glance showed him bare feet and brown legs beneath a fluffy white towel. He couldn't stop his gaze rising. The top of the towel was tucked firmly across the top of Sam's breasts and she had another towel wrapped around her head.

So she *had* been washing her hair…

'All yours,' Sam said cheerfully. 'It's a *great* shower.'

'Good.'

The need to get into the bathroom and lock the door behind him was so strong that Blake started moving a little more quickly than he'd intended. A single stride brought him right into Sam's path and she swerved to avoid him. Only he swerved as well, at the same moment and in the same direction.

It was a moment that held the same kind of awkwardness that it did on a crowded pavement. Like a dance move that had gone wrong. If they both moved again, it was highly likely that they'd do it all over again, so Blake froze to let Sam choose which way to go.

Only she froze as well.

And there they were. Face to face. Staring at each other as if the rest of the world had just ceased to exist. Wearing nothing but towels that could be removed with a single, casual flick of a hand.

Whatever simmering attraction or interest or whatever it was between them had suddenly exploded into a wildfire that was becoming more out of control with every passing heartbeat.

Blake was certainly losing any ability to control whatever was happening here. He couldn't even *think* about how to make his body move. He was drowning in the scent of Sam's skin, the warmth he could feel coming from her and…what looked like a mirror of his own desire being reflected back from eyes that had darkened to a blue more intense than anything he'd ever seen before.

His voice sounded weird. So strained he couldn't recognise it.

'This…can't happen.'

She was holding his gaze. Her voice came out in a husky whisper.

'Not even…once?'

It was like a 'get out of jail free' card being offered. A one-off. A way to satisfy what was the worst craving he'd ever experienced and for there not to be any consequences.

And Sam wanted it as much as he did?

His voice went from strained to hoarse.

'Just once?'

'Mmm…'

'And what happens here…stays here?'

'Absolutely.'

Sam caught her bottom lip with her teeth as if she was trying not to smile. And then she released it slowly and that was it. Blake lost any vestige of common sense. His gaze was locked onto her lips but he could sense the way her eyelids fluttered shut as he lowered his head to kiss her. The towel around her hair came loose as she tilted her head back to meet his mouth with hers. Long strands of damp hair cascaded over his arm as he cradled her head with his hand but it didn't dampen the fire of desire in any way.

If anything, it made it even hotter.

Nothing had ever felt like this before.

That gentleness with which her head was being cradled made Sam feel like a precious piece of china but the strength in those hands told her that Blake Cooper had a control over his body that was the sexiest thing she'd ever been aware of.

And then his lips touched hers and a very different kind of sensation pushed everything else into non-existence. A featherlike brush and then another and then his lips settled on hers and the first touch of his tongue sparked a flash of need so powerful it was actually scary.

She shouldn't be doing this and perhaps that heightened this desire. She'd never really rebelled in her life. Well…not since Alistair's tragic death, anyway. She'd kept herself safe. Chosen safe boyfriends and resisted any pull towards someone like Blake.

A maverick.

A bad boy.

Someone with whom a relationship would be unthinkable.

But this wasn't the opening dance of any kind of relationship. This was a one-off. Two adults who'd discovered an overpowering attraction for each other that needed...sating.

This was going to be the only time Sam would experience something like this—an encounter that was pretty much in forbidden territory.

And, dammit, she was going to make the most of it.

She kissed Blake back, her tongue tangling with his, a groan of desire coming from her own throat that she might have been embarrassed by in her old life.

Her fingers caught in the now dishevelled ponytail at the back of his head, so she pulled the band free and then raked her fingers through that delicious length of his hair. She pressed herself against the bare skin of his chest and inhaled the musky scent of unwashed maleness. Her hands were moving without any conscious direction now, slipping down his chest to the knot in that towel. It took only a swift tug for it to fall free and this time the groan came from Blake's throat.

A sexy growl that brought a huff of sound like laughter from Sam. And then she squeaked as he broke the passionate kiss only to scoop her up into his arms, carry her to the bed in just a couple of long strides, and practically throw her onto it. The move to pull her towel free a moment later was just as smooth and then, for a long moment, Blake seemed to freeze—simply staring down as he knelt over her.

Her own gaze was just as caught—by the naked, totally ripped and totally aroused body looming over her own.

She'd never seen anything so beautiful.

This was fantasy sex that was about to get very, very real and she'd never wanted anything as much as this.

But then her gaze lifted and locked with a set of dark, dark eyes.

This wasn't just sex, was it?

She was with *Blake*…

The most extraordinary man she'd ever met.

So it wasn't simply sex. This was a connection that suddenly felt overwhelmingly significant.

But she couldn't let Blake know that. She had promised that this was a one-off encounter, never to be mentioned again. It had to be simply about the sex.

So she smiled slowly. Lifted her hands to his head and pulled him down towards her, closing her eyes as she did so, so he wouldn't see anything that wasn't supposed to be a part of this.

When he bypassed her lips to go straight to her breasts, Sam let her head fall back against the pillows as she cried out in ecstasy. Who knew that the touch of a hand or lips or a tongue could be capable of creating such a powerful mix of bliss but also a need for more.

For everything.

She wanted a closer touch. She wanted to feel Blake right inside her. But she also wanted this to last for ever. To build and build this exquisite wanting, until the culmination would be the closest thing to paradise that could be found on earth.

And it was.

For the longest time, a long time later, Sam could only lie in Blake's arms, waiting for her pounding heart to settle and her gasping to become normal breathing again. She had no idea how long they'd been making love but, if they'd missed their flight, she couldn't have cared less.

Maybe the fact that so much of their skin was still in contact gave Blake an avenue for some kind of telepathy because she felt the movement of his arm as he tilted his wrist to glance at his watch.

The sound he made was like someone hearing the alarm clock sound when all they wanted to do was roll over and go back to a deep sleep.

'We need to get moving,' he murmured. 'I'm going to grab a quick shower and then we need to go and check in.' He kissed Sam's shoulder as he peeled himself away from her body. 'Or do you want another shower first?'

'I'm okay.' Sam kept her eyes closed. 'I can wait till I get home.'

Because that way, she could keep the scent of Blake's skin on her own for a little longer?

He swung his feet to the floor and got up. Took a step towards the bathroom but then paused and looked back. The half-smile and raised eyebrow was an unspoken question.

Another heartbeat and then he spoke, sounding almost surprised.

'You know, don't you?'

Sam let out her breath. 'Yeah... I know. What happened here stays here. I get it. It's fine.'

But he shook his head. 'You know how gorgeous you are, don't you?'

Sam shrugged. Managed a smile. 'You're not so bad yourself, mate.'

A wave of what felt like disappointment dimmed the glow she'd been basking in as she lay there for a minute longer, listening to the sound of the shower running.

This had only been a physical attraction for Blake, hadn't it? It wasn't that she was hoping for more—he'd made it very clear that this was just going to be a one-off sexual encounter and she *was* fine with that. It wasn't as if she was looking for a relationship with anyone and, if she was, he'd be the last person she would have chosen.

Perhaps the disappointment came from realising that he was more like every other man than she'd recognised. He wasn't such a maverick, after all.

And, if she was honest, her attraction to him had been purely physical at first, too. But something had changed over the course of this weekend. She'd seen beneath the gorgeous package. To a man who walked alone.

And possibly didn't even realise how lonely he was.

CHAPTER SIX

WHAT HAD HAPPENED there had stayed there.

And it was easier than Blake could have anticipated.

Okay, it felt a little weird when his path had crossed with Sam's in the corridor outside Emergency on that first Monday morning back at work. He'd avoided all but the most fleeting eye contact and had merely nodded and greeted her the way he would any other colleague, without breaking his forward movement in any way.

She'd been just as casual.

So casual, in fact, that Blake was left wondering for a moment if that steamy encounter in his hotel room had actually happened. Or had he dreamed it?

It certainly felt like a dream in retrospect.

The sexiest damn dream he'd ever had in his life.

The fantasy sex had lived up to any expectations he might have been harbouring. Exceeded them, in fact.

The level of ultimate satisfaction that had stayed with him for the journey home and right through the night had convinced him that it had been the right thing to do. He didn't have to wonder any more what it would be like to have the most beautiful woman he'd ever seen in his bed. What her skin felt like. Tasted like. What it would feel like to have her touching him. What tiny sounds of need or pleasure or ecstasy she might make...

Now he knew.

And that was that.

They could go back to working in the same department just as they had been before the USAR course weekend. Albeit with a secret between them but Blake was not a stranger to such secrets. Sam had just joined a club he wasn't particularly proud of—the women who worked at this hospital that he'd become a little more than friendly with for a brief time.

It seemed to work very well for that first

day. And for the next couple of days. But then Blake began to notice something different.

The fantasy sex hadn't stayed in that hotel room.

It was haunting his dreams.

It was in his head, refusing to be compartmentalised into a place that was merely a memory that he could choose—or choose not—to revisit.

The memory popped into his consciousness at unexpected moments. Like when he saw Sam in the department, going past wheeling an IV stand, for example. Or simply standing still, checking the patient board to see what patients she'd been assigned, like she was right now.

It was stronger when he heard the sound of her voice when he walked past a cubicle she was working in. Even worse, when he heard the sound of her laughter. He'd heard that delicious gurgle under such very different circumstances and he'd had to curl his fingers the first time he'd heard it again because they just itched to tickle her in a place where her skin was so incredibly soft and sensitive.

It should be getting easier to get past what

they'd both agreed was no more than a one-night stand.

But it was getting more and more irritating that, for the first time ever, he wasn't quite managing to.

Maybe it was because Sam seemed to have done it without any effort at all. In the past, he'd always caught lingering looks from such partners. They'd appeared in his path far more often than could be coincidental. There'd been tears, even. Or, they had gone out of their way to avoid him and, if they couldn't, he'd be on the receiving end of a death glare.

Not Sam. She was here, doing her job, day after day. Competent, cheerful and exactly the way she'd been before their time together. Nobody would ever guess what had happened in Brisbane and it seemed like it *hadn't* ever happened as far as Sam was concerned.

Perhaps that was what was really bothering him. Not that he couldn't move on and forget it but that Sam already had because it had meant nothing.

It was getting harder with every passing day.

How crazy had it been to think that 'just

once' would have been enough. That she could have walked away from that hotel room in Brisbane and been able to pretend that it had never happened.

Sam had known that it would be a bit weird on that Monday morning, the first time she saw Blake again, but she hadn't expected how devastating it would feel when he'd just walked past her in the corridor with a polite nod and barely a glance.

As crushing as anything that had happened back in those teenage years when she had been learning the hard way that dreams of finding true love and living happily ever after were exactly that—only dreams.

She had held her head high, however, and, if her smile had felt a little forced for the rest of that day with both her colleagues and her patients, it had been even brighter than usual. Nobody could have guessed the way her skin prickled at catching a glimpse of Blake on the other side of the department, or the deep twist in her gut when she heard the sound of his voice.

It wasn't as if she was allowing herself to remember how it felt to be touched by this man—not in the daytime, anyway. Nights were a very different story. No, it was more like he had touched every cell in her body and the awareness was no more controllable than, say, being aware of heat if you stepped into direct sunshine on a summer's day.

It should have got easier as the days went by but, if anything, that awareness was growing stronger. Getting laced with a longing to do it all again...

Sam thought she was hiding the struggle perfectly well but Harriet wasn't fooled by that overly bright smile when she finally caught up with her friend for a lunch break a few days into that week.

'What's up?' Harriet asked as they found a shady tree in the grounds to sit beneath to eat their sandwiches.

'Nothing.' Sam tried to look surprised.

She wanted to confess to her best friend— of course she did. But Harriet had warned her about Blake, hadn't she? She'd said nobody got close to him and those who tried only ended up with a broken heart. She'd be able to say 'I told you so' and Sam would have to agree. She'd have to admit she'd been stupid and, if she started feeling ashamed of herself, she'd feel even worse than she did now. On top of that, the memory of that extraordinary experience would be tarnished and it would change how it made her feel when she lay in her own bed and relived every moment.

And Harriet was part of the SDR team. Sam knew she would keep a secret if asked but what if it just slipped out somehow by a knowing glance or something? If certain other people knew, it might damage her chances of joining the team. Who would want someone on the team that might have an ulterior motive of distracting the team leader?

So she smiled at Harriet again and then shrugged. 'I guess I'm still a bit tired. That USAR course was full on and I've been working every day since.'

Harriet nodded. 'Of course. Sorry, I haven't had the chance to talk to you about it what with being so wrapped up with my new flatmate.' She rolled her eyes. 'I'm a bad friend.'

'Don't be daft. This is a special time for you and Pete. That's why I didn't call *you*.'

That wasn't quite the truth, though, was it? If she'd spoken to Harriet before the thrill of that encounter with Blake had been dented by his dismissive attitude at work, she might well have confessed everything, even knowing that she would have had to field the 'I told you so' response.

'I remember how full on it is. But did you like it?'

'Are you kidding? I *loved* it. Every moment of it.'

Some more than others, mind you. Sam chewed the inside of her cheek for a moment, focusing on peeling the seal from the plastic triangle that contained her sandwiches. It would be weird if she didn't mention who the instructor had been but this was going to be a real test of how well she could keep her own secret.

'You won't believe it, but the instructor was Blake Cooper.'

'No way... In *Brisbane*?'

'He was filling in for someone who'd been injured.'

'Wow. That must have been...um...interesting?'

'Mmm.' A mouthful of bread, tuna and mayonnaise was a great way of avoiding giving anything away.

'I'll bet he was surprised to see you there.'

'Mmm.'

'Was he nice to you?'

'He made me work hard. But…yeah…he was nicer than I expected him to be. Phew…' Sam reached for her water bottle when what she really wanted to do was fan her face with her hand. 'It's hot today, isn't it?'

'Sure is. So did you pass the test?'

'A hundred per cent.'

'Go, you. That'll be a feather in your cap when you decide to apply to join the team.'

'I hope so.'

'So when are you going to do it?'

'Um…not just yet.'

Oddly, making the team wasn't first and foremost in her thoughts currently. Blake Cooper had taken that spot. And she couldn't get her name put forward in the immediate aftermath of sleeping with one of the key people responsible for that decision, could she? It might make it seem like that was the only reason she'd encouraged that one-night stand. As if she was the kind of girl who thought sleeping her way to the top was acceptable.

And it might work against her, anyway. If Blake wanted to ignore her and pretend that it had never happened, he might be inclined to keep her out of the team just to underline the fact that it had meant nothing to him. That *she* meant nothing to him…

She could wait. Until it was no more than a memory for her, as well.

She needed to take a leaf out of Blake's book, that was all. If he could simply enjoy a night of the most incredible sex ever and then walk away as if it had never happened, then so could she.

And that might impress him just as much as proving herself clinically capable or acing a test and practical exercise in a completely different arena.

What was it they said? Fake it till you make it?

She was coping pretty well so far, given that Harriet didn't seem the least bit suspicious. Surely Blake must be just as convinced already. Who knew that those drama classes at high school would end up actually being rather useful?

'I will apply,' she told Harriet. 'But, for now, I'll just let Blake think about how well I did in that course.'

And about what had happened afterwards?

Surely he thought about that occasionally? Unless sex for him was always that mind blowing and she hadn't been anything out of the ordinary as far as he was concerned?

She dropped the last part of her sandwich back into the container. Her appetite had vanished.

I'll know when to pick the right time,' she told Harriet. 'Now...tell me about *your* weekend. What did you and Pete get up to? Some surfing? A fun run or something? Or were you both working?'

It was inevitable that they would end up having to work closely together.

At least he'd had more than a week to prepare for it but Blake hadn't expected to have to be quite *this* close. The department was stretched and the trauma team was already fully occupied with three victims from a motorway pile-up when another trauma case got wheeled through the ambulance bay doors. He was the consultant who stepped out from the resuscitation bays to assess the new arrival.

And Sam was the nurse standing beside the bed in the treatment room. She was arranging pillows to support the heavily bandaged arm and hand of a middle-aged man.

At least the paramedics were still here, packing up their gear.

'This is Stuart,' one of them told him. 'Fifty-eight years old. He got his arm caught in a conveyor belt at the factory he works in. De-gloving injury to his forearm and hand. Possible fracture. We've just covered it in sterile dressings and splinted it.'

The subtle shake of the paramedic's head warned Blake that the injury was severe.

'Vital signs?'

'All recorded on arrival and en route. GCS has been fifteen throughout. Sinus tachycardia. Sats normal.'

'Pain relief?'

'He's got five milligrams of morphine on board, which seemed to do the trick.'

'Past medical history?'

'He's diabetic. On beta blockers for hypertension and he's a smoker.'

Blake's heart sank a little. They could all complicate the road to successful treatment, especially if delicate surgery was required.

'I can't lose my hand,' Stuart was saying to Sam as the paramedics left. 'Please... I've got six kids at home and my job's the only thing keeping us afloat. You've got to help me...'

'We'll do everything we can.' Her voice was reassuring. 'You're lucky, Stuart.' She was smiling at her patient now. 'You've scored the best doctor we've got at Bondi Bay. This is Blake Cooper…'

'G'day, Stuart.' Blake stepped closer to the bed. It was disconcerting that he had to make a conscious effort to chase the effects of hearing Sam's voice up close into the back of his head. And that smile…

Thank goodness he had a patient to focus on.

'I'm going to give you a quick all-over check first and make sure we're not missing any other injuries and then we'll take a good look at that arm of yours, okay?'

Sam was just as focused. She had wrapped a blood pressure cuff around Stuart's uninjured arm and was checking the IV line to make sure they still had a vein open if needed. She had both the ECG and drug trolleys nearby as well.

A few minutes later and it was time to unwrap the bandages and remove the dressings applied at the scene.

'You don't need to look,' Sam said to Stuart. 'Sometimes it's better not to.'

It was probably just as well that Stuart chose to turn his head away and close his eyes. De-gloving injuries, where the skin was pulled away from underlying structures of muscle and bone, were usually horrendous and this was no exception.

The forearm was stripped to the wrist and the little finger of Stuart's hand was simply bone. The ring and middle finger at least had some muscle still attached and there was an ooze of blood providing reassurance that blood vessels were still intact.

'Can you move your fingers, Stuart?'

The movement was creepily normal so nerves were still intact as well. It was like watching an anatomical model come to life.

Blake flicked his gaze upwards. Even people used to dealing with traumatic injuries could find something like this confronting and he needed to know if Sam could handle it.

Her gaze met his. He could see that she was shocked. He could also see that she could cope. That she was trusting him to know what to do and that she would do whatever was needed to assist him.

And suddenly there was no danger of being

distracted by any thoughts about Samantha Braithwaite that were decidedly unprofessional. He had a colleague here that he knew was competent and that he could trust and... he wouldn't have wanted anyone else to be working with him right now.

They could do this.

'We're going to re-cover the wounds with saline-soaked dressings,' he told her. 'We need X-rays and Triple A therapy.'

Sam nodded. She already had a bowl of dressings ready. 'Analgesia, antibiotics and ADT if needed.' She turned her head. 'Stuart, have you had a tetanus vaccination recently?'

'Not that I can remember. How bad is it, Doc?'

'It's not pretty,' Blake said. 'But it could have been worse. I'm going to get some surgical specialists to come down and see you but we need to get some X-rays first to see if any bones are broken or whether any bits of that conveyor belt got left behind.'

'It was so stupid,' Stuart groaned. 'Something got stuck and I thought that I could just poke it with a stick, you know? The belt grabbed the stick so fast I didn't have time to let go. My wife's going to kill me...'

'Has someone got in touch with her for you?' Sam asked.

'Yeah…but she's got to find someone to look after the kids before she can come in. The twins are only three and they're a real handful, you know? Ahh…that *hurts*…'

'Can you draw up some more morphine, please, Sam? I think we need to top up that pain relief.'

'Got it here.' Sam handed him a syringe with the ampoule taped to the side so that he could check the dose and expiry date.

Man…she was impressive to work with. He had to smile as he thanked her and his gaze snagged hers for just an instant.

They were both being ultimately professional. Blake didn't doubt that in the least but he also knew that the beat of connection he was aware of had elements that went beyond anything he normally had, even with his most trusted colleagues.

Everything about Sam was just that little bit different, wasn't it?

His shift was officially over well before Stuart was passed into the care of the surgeons. Blake knew that Sam had also stayed on, having become so involved with this case. She looked after Marie, Stuart's wife, after she arrived and sat with her as decisions were made about the best course of treatment. X-rays and clinical photographs had been taken and Blake's initial overall examination had been followed up with investigations on all of Stuart's existing medical conditions. The time off work that would be needed for complex reconstructive surgery that could potentially save all his fingers had to be taken into account as well, given that he was the sole financial support for his family.

'I don't care,' Stuart finally decided. 'If losing my little finger and half my ring finger means I can get back to work sooner, that's what I'll do. I'll still be able to use my hand well enough, I reckon.'

'If you stop smoking, you'll recover a lot better and faster,' the surgeon told him. 'It affects blood supply and healing time quite dramatically.'

'I've been telling him to stop for years,' Marie said. 'If losing a finger is what it takes then maybe this is worth it.' She had tears running down her face as she gripped her husband's uninjured hand. 'I can't lose you, Stu. I need you. The kids need you...'

'I'm sorry...' Stuart was crying as well. 'I'll never touch another cigarette, I promise. I love you, honey...'

The emotion in the room was enough to touch everybody. Sam was blinking hard as she walked past Blake, having wished Stuart all the best for the next steps in his recovery.

Perhaps she felt how intently he was watching her because she turned her head and caught his gaze.

And, just for a heartbeat, he saw something unguarded.

Something that suggested a connection that had absolutely nothing to do with the case they'd just spent so much time working on together. Something that made him think Sam knew too much about love...and grief...

It was only the briefest moment of eye contact but it was enough for Blake to realise that pretending nothing had happened between them wasn't going to work any more. Whether he liked it or not, there was something there that wasn't going to fade by being ignored.

If anything, the curiosity and...and this

astonishing pull to be close to Sam was just going to get worse.

He was going to have to try something else.

The opportunity to do that came when he fortuitously caught up with Sam as she was walking towards the car park, having finally clocked off.

Okay…so maybe he'd planned his route so that that was going to happen but his decision had been made in that moment of eye contact as she'd left the treatment room.

Maybe it was due to the relief that it was clearly possible to work with Sam without anything that had happened interfering with how professional they could be.

Or maybe it was because he had reached breaking point with not being able to get her out of his head.

Then again, maybe it was what he had seen in that glance that had made him simply want to take her into his arms and hold her close. Very, very close…

Whatever it was, something had to be done.

He needed to know whether what he'd thought he'd seen in her eyes meant that she was also aware of this feeling of connection and was experiencing the same kind of pull towards him or had Sam really moved on without a second thought or backward glance? If she had, fine, he would do the same. Somehow.

But if she hadn't…

Well… Hopefully, he'd know what he wanted to do about that when he knew how things stood.

Sam had known that Blake Cooper was a smooth operator but there was something about the way he appeared so casually and fell into step beside her that made her suspicious that it wasn't entirely a coincidence.

Had he planned this?

Why…because he wanted to talk to her in private?

Her heart stumbled for a beat and then picked up its pace. Her awareness of Blake in a purely professional setting was hard enough to handle sometimes. Walking side by side, she found that awareness was almost unbearable. She didn't dare catch his gaze.

'Thanks for staying on,' Blake said. 'Stuart's wife really appreciated your support.'

'I couldn't leave without knowing what's

coming next for them. Do you think amputation was the best choice?'

'I do. Losing a little finger will have minimal effect on his ability to use his hand and, if the replantation and revascularisation of the other areas is successful, he might get full cover for the length of time he'll have to be away from work.'

'It's going to be a tough time for the family.'

'It is.' Sam could feel Blake looking down at her as they neared her car. 'But families can survive if they stick together. If there's enough love...'

Sam swallowed hard. 'I think there is...' She had stopped walking now. She couldn't not look up to meet his gaze. 'Don't you?'

Oh, wow...

Talk about falling into someone's eyes. Maybe it was the echoes of the 'L' word hanging in the air between them.

How was she supposed to keep this casual? To pretend that what had happened had been left behind in that hotel room and forgotten?

But...perhaps she didn't have to...

That *look*... She'd seen it once before. When they had been lying in bed together.

When Blake had been poised above her and right about to...

He cleared his throat.

'I...ah... I've been thinking,' he said slowly.

'Me, too,' she whispered back.

'About...you know...'

'Mmm.' Sam could feel colour seeping into her cheeks. 'I know.'

Blake glanced around, as if checking that no one was within earshot. 'And I know we agreed that it was a one-off, but...'

But?

Sam's balance suddenly felt a bit off kilter. As if her legs didn't want to hold her up any more. She focused on Blake's feet to steady herself. On those stupid, sexy cowboy boots.

'I don't do...relationships,' he muttered then.

'Neither do I,' Sam heard herself say.

And it was true, although not because it wasn't something she *wanted*. Eventually. Was it possible that it was the same for Blake? Did he think he wasn't relationship material simply because nothing had worked for him so far? What was holding him back?

She had to catch his gaze again and she knew that her curiosity would be evident.

What surprised her was seeing a reflection of that curiosity in *his* gaze.

'It was a one-off for more than the fact that neither of us do relationships,' she said. 'We work together. It would be unprofessional.'

Blake snorted softly. 'It's pretty unprofessional to be thinking about it all the time.'

Again, Sam seemed to see her own thoughts reflected in those dark eyes. He had been finding this as difficult as she had? Wow...

'And my reputation is bad enough already, I believe.'

She had to smile. 'I believe so, too.' She caught her lip between her teeth. 'So, it wouldn't really change anything, then...'

'No.'

Could Blake hear how hard her heart was thumping right now? 'Um...maybe we just need to get it out of our system, then.'

His voice was a low, sexy rumble. 'Are you suggesting what I think you're suggesting? Another...one-off?'

Sam shrugged, trying to cover the wash of excitement running through her body. Trying to make this seem not a big deal.

'Or a two-off. A three-off, if that's what it takes.' She took a deep breath and then held his gaze steadily as she gathered her words. Yes, she did want a real relationship that was going somewhere but it had to be with the right person and that person wasn't going to be Blake Cooper because she could sense that his demons were even bigger than hers.

But, oh…that didn't stop the *wanting*, did it? The lure of the bad boy…

'We both walk alone, Blake,' she said quietly, 'for whatever reason—and at some point we'll know it's enough. Maybe we just need to agree that when one of us reaches that point, the other walks away too. No regrets. No looking back.'

Somehow, she had moved closer to Blake as she'd been speaking, without realising it. Her head was tilted up so that she could hold his gaze and he was looking down.

Leaning down…as if he couldn't resist the urge to kiss her.

Then he straightened suddenly and Sam could feel the distance increasing between them with a wave of disappointment. Despair, almost…?

But he was smiling. That crooked, irresistibly charming smile of a man who knew exactly what he wanted and was quite confident he was going to get it.

'What are you doing tonight, Sam?'

Her mouth felt dry. 'Nothing important.'

'Give me your address and I'll come and get you. You up for a bike ride?'

Sam could almost hear her mother shrieking in horror at the thought but her rebellious streak wasn't about to be quashed. She might only get one more night with this man so why not add an extra thrill to it?

She could feel her smile stretching into a grin. 'Bring it on.'

CHAPTER SEVEN

WELL...

This was a bit of a turnaround.

Blake had always been the one to call the shots when it came to applying boundaries to any kind of relationships. He was the one to make it clear that it was never going to be anything long term and he was always the one to call 'time' when it was over.

It seemed like he had met his match because there was a real possibility that, this time, it would be Sam who decided when enough was enough.

And it was making him feel...competitive?

He was going to give Sam Braithwaite a night to remember. One that would—hopefully—have her begging for more.

Or maybe it was more a need to gain the usual kind of control he had over situations like this. If she wanted more, he would be back in the driver's seat and he could decide when it was time to pull the plug on this connection.

Whatever…it was a slightly disconcerting position to be in but to walk away from an offer of more of the best sex he'd ever had in his life with no strings attached? An impossible ask.

Could that mean he had already lost control?

Blake pushed that alarming notion into a headspace that he wasn't about to revisit. It was nonsense. If he really wanted to escape, he could end this at any time, however difficult it might be.

He just *didn't* want to. Not yet.

Speeding over the Sydney Harbour bridge later that night, with the sparkling lights of this beautiful city reflected in the expanse of water and Sam's arms tightly wound around his waist and her body pressing against his back, made Blake realise just how much he didn't want this to end.

He wanted this particular night to last for ever.

He knew the best restaurant, with a harbour view. Well, okay, it was only a café but that meant it didn't matter that they were wearing jeans. And it did have the best blues band he'd heard in a long time and he had a feeling that Sam might be up for a bit of dancing.

Slow dancing.

A kind of foreplay that could last for hours and build desire until it was unbearable for both of them.

Who would crack first and suggest that it was time to go home?

He'd changed the sheets on the big bed in the corner of his loft apartment. He'd even thought to put a bunch of candles nearby, ready to provide the kind of romantic light that would be just enough to see every delicious curve of Sam's body. To see the expression in her eyes when he took them both to paradise…

Oh, man…

He was going to crack first, wasn't he? Slowing for some traffic lights on the other side of the bridge, it took a surprising amount of self-control not to turn the bike around right then.

Instead he turned his head.

'You good?'

Sam's gloved fingers pressed more deeply into his abdomen. Her voice might be raised but it was still the sexiest sound he'd ever heard.

'Never better… Can we go a bit faster?'

She'd died and gone to bad boy heaven, that's what this was.

Right from the moment she'd walked out of the door of her apartment block and there he'd been. Sitting there, astride that big bike—like a modern-day Marlon Brando—holding out her helmet and gloves like an invitation to step into her fantasy world.

The sensation of speed, with her body exposed to the elements, was a thrill that was poignant because it gave her an unexpected jolt of connection with the big brother she missed so much. Finally, she could understand his love for this mode of transport— this heady mix of delight and danger. It made her tighten her hold on Blake's body and that gave her another kind of jolt. A feeling of safety.

No…it was more complex than that. She knew this was dangerous but, because she was with Blake, she simply didn't care. She was quite prepared to go anywhere he wanted to lead her.

Even if it turned out it was only for one more night.

She'd expected him to be taking her to where he lived. To where there was a private space with a bed. That was what this was all about, wasn't it?

Just sex. An attraction that apparently neither of them had had enough of yet.

But it seemed that Blake had other ideas.

The smoky, dimly lit, seaside café bar was a place she'd never heard of and probably would never have thought to enter even if she had, to be honest. But the garlic prawns and fries they ate with their fingers was the most delicious food ever. And the dancing...

Who knew that Blake Cooper was capable of dancing like this? It was just as well this place was so dimly lit, because it almost felt like they were making love with their clothes on. Every stroke of his hand down her back that ended in his cupping her bottom. Every press of his forehead against hers so that she could feel his breath on her face. Sam never wanted it to stop.

But she wanted it to stop right now. So they could go somewhere and be alone. To do what had been the intention of suggesting another 'one-off' and sate the need to be with each other in the most intimate way possible.

Blake didn't seem to be in any hurry, however. His body language was totally relaxed but, as the evening wore on, it didn't quite match the intensity she could feel in his gaze.

Finally, she couldn't stand it any longer. She twisted in his arms on the dance floor so that she could see his face properly.

'What time does this place close?'

'I think it stays open all night.'

Okay, there was a twinkle in that intensity now and Sam realised that he'd been playing with her. Waiting…

She shifted her hold, snaking one hand up to thread her fingers into his hair and pull his head close enough to touch her lips against his. Just the softest graze of contact and she kept her eyes open so that she could catch the moment he knew he'd lost whatever game he'd been playing.

He almost pushed her in his haste to leave the dance floor but that only made it impossible for Sam to hide her smile.

* * *

Not tonight. Busy.

Blake stared at the three words he had just tapped into his phone. His finger hovered over the 'send' button.

It would be the first time in nearly a month that he hadn't moved heaven and earth to try and make it possible to spend time with Sam.

And it was his mother's fault.

Okay, maybe an alarm bell had sounded a while back—after the third or fourth time, perhaps—when neither of them seemed at all inclined to walk away.

Why would they? The sex was fantastic and they enjoyed each other's company. There were no strings attached. Not even a heavy conversation that pried into his past or demanded forecasts concerning his future. It didn't make any difference to how well they worked together, either. He wasn't subjected to lingering, hopeful glances or 'accidental' meetings and Sam clearly hadn't told anybody about their arrangement because nobody had said anything. He hadn't even noticed a raised eyebrow from Emily's direction.

It felt like a game. Like the one he'd instigated on that first night, when he'd been teasing her on the dance floor and trying to make her crack first and suggest they go somewhere more private.

He'd lost that time. The stakes might be a little higher now but Blake didn't want to lose this time.

It was Sam's turn to crack first. She needed to be the one to walk away.

He'd expected it to have happened by now. They'd had their fun, hadn't they?

Alarm bells couldn't be ignored this time, thanks to his mother. Maybe Emily hadn't noticed anything different at work but Sharon Cooper wasn't so easily fooled.

'So, who is she this time?'

'What do you mean?'

'I know that look. It's not just that I haven't seen so much of you lately. You've got… I don't know…a sort of glow.'

Blake snorted. 'A *glow*? Good grief…'

Sharon sighed. 'You look happier, that's all. And that's a good thing.' She smiled as she got slowly to her feet to carry her plate to the sink. 'Maybe this time I'll get to meet her.'

And that's when it happened.

For the first time ever, Blake actually

wanted to bring a girl home to meet his mother.

He'd been planning to text her after his visit here and see if she was free later tonight. But Sam had texted first to ask if *he* was free and the timing couldn't have been worse because the message had pinged onto his phone as he was sitting there, shocked at the very idea of inviting his current bed partner into his very private life.

Maybe he just had to take it on the chin and let Sam win again this time.

He was going to crack first.

It took just a tiny tap to send his text message on its way.

Now all he had to do was ease his conscience by making sure he *was* busy later. There were a couple of odd jobs that needed doing for his mother but, after that, Blake decided he would head to the gym. He hadn't had a good workout for far too long.

Not the sort you could do in public, anyway.

It was Harriet's fault.

Sam stood at the bottom of the most daunting climbing wall she'd ever seen but the impressive variety of overhangs and cracks wasn't what was making this so very difficult.

She'd had a go at indoor climbing before and loved it but it was a long time ago and the person who'd been her belayer had been her brother, Alistair. It had been unthinkable to go back without him. Or to play at the type of activity that had led to his death.

What she was grappling with now, as she clipped her belay device to the carabiner on her harness, was a weird mix of emotions.

A wave of grief for Alistair but a sense of pride, as well. She knew that he'd be applauding her right now. Or giving her a thumbs-up, anyway. For being courageous. For breaking through such a huge barrier.

For being so determined not to let it bother her that she couldn't be with Blake Cooper tonight and then doing something about it by grabbing her keys and heading straight out the door.

She wouldn't have thought of coming here in a million years, though, if she hadn't just had that conversation with Harriet.

'I've just had an email about the next training day for the SDR,' she'd told Sam. 'It's a rock-climbing exercise. Didn't you do that when you were a teenager?'

'It's so long ago, I've probably forgotten everything.'

'Nah… I'll bet it's like riding a bike. Muscle memory, you know? Maybe you could get a practice session in first, just to make sure, but I reckon it's the perfect time to put your name forward to try out. Want me to do it?'

Sam's phone sounded her text alert and she put Harriet on speaker phone so that she could change screens, knowing that it could be Blake answering her text.

Not tonight. Busy.

No apology. No suggestion of another day.

It felt like a dismissal. Was this how he was choosing to let her know that it was over?

If it was, there was nothing she could do about it. They'd made an agreement, hadn't they? When one of them reached that point, the other had to simply walk away too. No regrets. No looking back.

Where on earth had this wash of *fear* come from?

It wasn't as if she was in love with Blake. This had been supposed to be fun. A fantasy with the bad boy who broke everybody's hearts.

It certainly wasn't supposed to be threatening to break *her* heart.

And she wouldn't let it.

'Sam? You still there?'

She tuned back in to Harriet's voice. 'Yes... sorry... I was just thinking.'

'That it's time? I can put the wheels in motion for you to get a try out for the team.'

'You know what? I think you're right. And seeing as I haven't got anything better to do tonight, I'm going to go to that gym near the hospital and see what their climbing wall looks like.'

'Go, you. Hey, if you see Pete there, can you give him a message?'

'Sure.'

'Tell him his dinner's getting cold.' Harriet laughed. 'And I'm getting hot.'

There'd been no sign of Pete when Sam had arrived and organised her climbing session and gear rental. She now had a harness on over her soft yoga pants and sports top, soft climbing shoes with grippy soles and a new chalk ball that she would use to keep her fingers and palms dry.

An instructor checked her harness and clipped the belay device to her carabiner. Her rope was also attached to an overhead anchor because she was doing what was called 'top roping'.

'Are you sure about using the auto belay? Seeing as it's your first time here, it might be better to have someone on the other end of the rope. If you can wait thirty minutes, I've got a free slot.'

'I'll have a go,' Sam told him. 'I have done it before and I'll just go the easiest route. That's the green holds, yes?'

'Yeah... Green, then orange and the most difficult is red. Easy to remember, like traffic lights. You sure you're okay with heights?'

Sam took a deep breath as she glanced up at just how high this wall was. It was safe, she reminded herself. If she missed a hold she could only fall a short distance before the belay device would lock the rope. It might be embarrassing but she wasn't going to get anything more than a bump or a graze from the textured material that looked remarkably like natural rocks. She grinned at the staff member.

'Soon find out, I guess.'

'If you get stuck, someone will be able to help. Main thing is not to panic.'

'Got it. Thanks for your help.'

'I'll check on you. Offer's still open for a training session later if you want it.'

The first few holds were easy with good-sized pegs coming out from the wall or boulders that had plenty of room for a foot or hand hold. Sam took it slowly and carefully but it seemed no time at all before she was quite a long way from ground level.

She didn't look down, however. Or up. She remembered that from those sessions with Alistair so long ago. Her focus only needed to be on the next green marker. One step at a time. There were people here who were at the top of this game and they'd set this route. Beginner's level but it still required physical effort and a determined mind set.

Halfway up the wall, Sam wobbled, clinging to the wall like a crab and pausing to take several steadying, deep breaths.

This was a lot harder than climbing over a huge pile of debris and remembering to keep three points of contact with the surface at all times. An image of Blake filled her head for a moment then, and Sam realised it was the first time she'd thought about him since she'd arrived at the gym.

That had to be a good thing, didn't it?

And maybe it would be a good thing if their time together *had* finished. It would mean less of a complication for when she joined the SDR team. She'd just have to learn to do without him in her life in other ways.

She'd just have to get over this fear that it might be a lot more difficult than she might have expected.

Like this climb was threatening to be now that she wasn't concentrating.

Sam forced herself to focus. *You can do this*, she told herself firmly. *Imagine that it's Alistair holding your rope. That he's yelling at you now to get on with the next hold. Asking if you've fallen asleep or something...*

The thought made her smile. Glance down for a heartbeat, even, as though she would really see her brother down there.

What she did see were other people on the wall below her. Someone was bouldering with no ropes, on a route close to the floor with crash mats beneath them. And someone else was lead climbing where they clipped their rope onto a series of points bolted to the wall rather than overhead. It was a lot harder than top roping and this person was using the red markers as well.

Clearly an expert. For a moment, he was hidden by an overhang and all Sam could see were his fingers as he found a grip that would be enough to haul his body weight through space until he could hook a foot over the edge.

Wow…

If he lost his grip, he'd fall to where the previous clip point was and that could be enough to cause quite a serious injury.

She found she was holding her breath as the foot appeared and then muscles bulged in bare arms as more of his body appeared and then twisted. For a moment, he was in a sitting position on the overhang, but he didn't pause to take a breath, instantly crouching and looking up to see where his new clip point or hold was.

Her breath came out in an incredulous huff. *Blake*?

Had she said his name aloud, or had he just heard it anyway?

Or was she just close enough to where his route was leading him?

Whatever. His gaze snagged on hers and then away again, as if he wasn't even surprised.

But he came sideways. As if it didn't matter in the least that he was choosing orange holds instead of red. Or that his clip point was getting further and further away.

'What the heck are *you* doing here?'

'Climbing a wall.'

'I've never seen you here before.'

'First time,' Sam admitted.

'And you're doing it by yourself?' Blake looked incredulous. 'Are you crazy?'

'I've done it before. I just wanted to see how much I remembered.'

'Why?'

For a moment, Sam completely forgot that she was a human spider quite a long way from a solid surface. She held Blake's gaze and tried not to fall into the pull she could feel from his body. From the sweat-slicked skin that his tank top left exposed. From that intense heat in his eyes.

'I heard that the next SDR training session involves some climbing. Harriet's going to put my name forward and I intend to be ready for it.'

The corner of Blake's mouth curled upwards as he shook his head. 'I've got to hand it to you, Sam. You don't give up when you want something, do you?'

'I don't expect you do, either.'

The smile vanished. 'Not unless I have to.'

Was he referring to his dream of joining MSF? Was it a warning, perhaps, that Sam might have to give up on joining the team because he had no intention of allowing her to try out for it?

She held his gaze for a moment longer. *You can't do that to me*, she told him silently. *It wouldn't be fair...*

'Everything okay up there?' The instructor who'd helped Sam had noticed their lack of movement.

'All good, Dave,' Blake called back. His gaze slid back to Sam. 'Or is it?'

'You tell me,' she said. 'Are you going to let me try out for the team?'

'Is that what you really want?' His voice was low. Sexy. As if he was asking about something she wanted him to do to her body and Sam found her lips parting. She had to dampen them with her tongue before she could respond.

'Yes,' she whispered. 'Yes, please…'

His gaze jerked away from hers. Shifted to a point on the wall she couldn't see. And then he started moving away from her. She heard his voice clearly enough, however.

'Guess we'll see you at the training session then.'

Yes…

The excitement his words generated was enough to have Sam conquering the last few holds on her route as if it had only been yesterday that she'd done anything like this. She was still some distance from the very top of the wall but this was the beginner's level and it was high enough. She needed to start going down now and that was going to be slower and harder.

Blake was right at the top. Tackling another overhang.

And, as Sam watched, he lost his grip. For a heart-stopping instant, he was swinging, holding onto the edge of the overhang with only one hand.

Okay, he was clipped in to one side of the obstacle and he wouldn't fall far but that didn't stop the trickle of horror that raced down Sam's spine.

The impact of knowing how she would feel if he got injured. Or killed…

And it was in that instant that she realised just how wrong she'd been.

She hadn't believed that she was in love with Blake Cooper?

Who the heck had she been trying to kid?

CHAPTER EIGHT

THE SMALL GROUP of people looked much bigger once they were clustered together in the limited space available on the top of this cliff.

Members of Bondi Bayside's specialist disaster relief team had carpooled out of Sydney to meet in the Blue Mountains and have an intensive day's training in abseiling under the direction of an outdoor sports education company—a combination of increasing their skill sets and a bonding exercise for the team.

As always, with training days and meetings they had been joined by people outside the core team of medics who were part of the available pool for emergencies and often worked closely with the team on any callouts. Harriet's boyfriend, Pete, was here and so was Jack Evans, a young paramedic who had joined at the same time as Harriet and was passionate about rescue work.

One person had a rather different goal, however. Samantha Braithwaite was here to try out for the team. Harriet had put her name forward and both Luc Braxton and Kate Mitchell hadn't hesitated to second the nomination. This was the opportunity for everybody to get to know her. To see what kind of skills she already had but, more importantly, what her attitude was like and how well she communicated with and respected the people who were already an integral part of the team.

And that was the only reason she was here.

'Does anyone need help with their Prusik loop?'

The extra loop of rope, secured by a double fisherman's knot to link the main rope to a harness, was sometimes called a 'dead man's handle' and it was an essential safety measure.

Sam was nearby and Jack was showing her how to wrap the loop around her rope and fasten it to the carabiner.

'Make sure you've locked it,' Blake told her.

Her glance flicked upwards. 'Sure.'

She looked nervous, he decided. But excited as well. He wanted to give her an encouraging smile. To tell her that she was amazing and she could do this.

Instead, he moved away to check Kate's harness.

Sam was not going to be treated any differently from anyone else who was trying out for the team. Whatever had been between them was over.

Sam's choice.

She'd told him that being on this team was the thing she wanted most of all.

Okay, maybe he hadn't spelt out that nothing could happen again between them on a personal level if she joined the SDR but everyone knew that he disapproved of relationships between team members because they had the potential to interfere with critical decision-making procedures. He was keeping an eye on how Pete and Harriet worked together these days and, if he noticed any hint of them being distracted by each other, he might have to suggest that one of them step away from the team.

And he had the feeling that Sam understood that.

The way she understood a lot of stuff he'd never actually talked about with her.

Like his private life—and his past—being exactly that. Private.

Like the fact that he was never going to have anyone else dependent on him. At some point in his future, although of course he hoped that it was a long way away, he was going to be completely free—to do what he wanted with his life, wherever that might be in the world. To create a new type of prison with a long-term relationship, let alone a wife and children, was unthinkable.

Blake moved past where Harriet and Luc were lining up to be amongst the first people to lower themselves down this cliff. They were laughing about something, totally at ease in each other's company, as good friends always were.

As he and Sam had been?

What about the other things she had understood about him?

Like how deep that driving need for as much freedom and independence as he could find was?

The way she made him feel valued and respected because of it?

The feeling that his life was bigger and better and so much more exciting when he was with her and could see himself reflected in her eyes.

The way she touched him. Not just physically, although missing that was an ache he couldn't escape from at the moment, but somewhere deep in his soul as well. A place that nobody other than his mother had ever really touched.

He hadn't expected to be missing her this much. The shock of wanting to take her home to meet his mother and the conviction that it was time to step away had worn off, taking with it the relief that Sam had made the first move to end things by choosing to try out for the team.

She hadn't texted him since. At work, it was like it had been when she'd first arrived, with no hint of anything personal in any interaction they had. She was professional and cheerful and…

And it had been killing him, inch by inch.

One of the instructors was coaching Harriet to climb carefully over the cliff edge and get into position for the descent.

'Keep your feet wide apart. One hand on

the rope above and the other is going to control your Prusik loop. Now lean back into your harness.'

She and Pete had been careful to stay away from each other as the team had prepared for this. If they could manage a serious relationship and both be part of this team, why couldn't he?

Because it wasn't an option, that's why.

The fact that he was even considering bending his own rules to accommodate more than a friendship with Sam as a team member was enough of a red flag. Besides, a serious relationship had never been a consideration, not only for him but for Sam as well. It had been a perfect alliance. Great sex—okay, the best sex *ever*—and not a single string.

So why did he have the disturbing sensation that he was still tied to this woman—not with a string that could be broken easily enough but with a rope heavy enough to anchor a damn battleship?

His problem. Sam didn't seem to be suffering.

If she made the grade and joined the team, she would probably have no issues with dismissing their shared history but, for the first time in his life, Blake was less confident that he could move on so easily.

It might be a relief if she didn't make the grade because keeping a professional distance would be easier in a controlled environment like the emergency department.

But the pull was still there. He *wanted* to see her. To work with her. To be reminded of the person he believed he was when she was close. And he didn't want to be any kind of obstacle to Sam becoming the person she wanted so much to be. She hadn't done anything wrong. Far from it. And she deserved to be treated with the same respect and fairness that he would treat anyone else who came to try out for the team.

Blake could feel the tension in his body.

He needed to step back and deal with his own conflict in his own time.

If Sam was good enough, she could be invited to be a part of this and he would cope. Somehow.

If she wasn't, she wouldn't be invited.

It was that simple.

Sam was one of the last people to take her turn abseiling down this cliff.

Was this a kindness on the part of the group—so that she could watch everybody else manage it and gain confidence for her own performance? Or, and she suspected this might be the case, would they all be down at the bottom watching and assessing how well she could cope with a challenge that was both physical and mental?

Harriet had been down for a long time now but Pete was only just climbing over the edge to take his turn.

The instructors here probably had no idea that those two were a couple but Sam had come here in their car and they'd explained why it would be like that.

'There's an unspoken rule that SDR members do not hook up with each other,' Harriet had said. 'And if they do, one of them might be expected to step down from the team.'

'Whose rule? No, let me guess… Blake Cooper's?'

'Yep.'

'But Pete isn't a staff member at Bondi Bayside. Why would the rule apply to him?'

'Because we go to the same callouts. Because personal relationships can influence decision making. Or be a distraction.'

'Yeah...' Pete had been smiling. 'Harriet might put herself in danger to save me at the expense of victims.'

Harriet had laughed. 'Or you might get overcome with lust and forget what it is you're supposed to be shoring up or something.'

'Happens all the time, babe.'

Sam had tuned out of their playful banter.

Was this why she hadn't heard a word from Blake ever since that night at the gym when he'd agreed to let her try out for the team? Why he seemed as distant as he had been when she'd first started working at Bondi Bayside?

Was that what the intensity had really been about? Had she been making a choice between being on the team and being with him?

Sam cast a quick glance over her shoulder to where Blake was chatting to one of the people who ran this outdoor education centre.

If she'd known that, would she have made the same choice?

The excitement of getting within touching distance of her goal of joining the team should have been enough to fill the gaping hole in her life that had appeared after that night at the gym.

But it wasn't.

'You all set?'

'I think so.'

'Let me just check all the locks on your carabiners.' The instructor reached for the big metal loop that was attaching Sam's belay plate to the centre of her harness. She couldn't help casting one more glance towards Blake. Any moment now and she would be stepping over that cliff.

In front of him. Even more than doing well enough to be invited to join this team, right now what Sam wanted most of all was for Blake to be proud of her.

It intensified the ache that had been with her for over a week now. The ache that was an apparently forlorn longing to be with him again. Not just physically—this went so much deeper than that.

How could she have made a choice between being with Blake Cooper and being on the team? In a way it was impossible to separate the two because, to Sam, Blake was the spirit of this team.

Independent. Intelligent. Brave.

The things she longed to be herself. To be brave enough to get rid of any of the shreds of that cotton wool she had wrapped herself in ever since Alistair had died.

Smart enough to keep herself as safe as possible when they were all gone.

And independent enough to cope with the fears of the people she loved—her parents—but not to let their fears make her less than the person she was capable of being.

So, even if she had known there was a choice, it wouldn't have been a simple one. And, if she could have been strong enough, the choice she needed to make would have still been the same. She would have chosen the team. Maybe being with Blake could have been enough to make her the person she wanted to be but it wouldn't have lasted, would it? He had only done what she had known he would do at some point. He had walked away for no obvious reason except that maybe they had become too close for his comfort.

If she made the team, at least that could last for as long as *she* needed, or wanted, it to.

'You're good to go,' the instructor told her. 'Let's get you over the edge.'

Cautiously, Sam sat on the edge of the cliff, her legs dangling. As she turned her body to lower herself and let her harness take her weight, she could see that Blake had stopped talking and he was watching her every move.

A split second of eye contact and then his lips curved into a smile so subtle that anyone else might not have noticed.

But Sam did.

And it cut straight through her nerves.

Okay…maybe she wouldn't have chosen the team.

She would have chosen even a little more time to be close to the man she loved *this* much…

Blake waited at the top of the cliff, hanging there in his harness, holding his ropes but looking down. The rest of the team were at the bottom of the cliff. Some were looking up, also watching, but others were moving away to get ready for their next challenge— a bit of bouldering.

Sam was doing well. A little cautious with her rope management, which made her slow, but that wasn't a bad thing.

She was about halfway down when Blake felt something odd.

A tremor that he could feel through his

ropes that were anchored to a bolt deep in a rock well back from this cliff face.

And then the instructor, who would be the last to follow this group down, let out a warning shout and threw himself sideways—away from the cliff edge.

An edge that Blake could see was crumbling.

Not much. It was just a medium-sized rock that was coming free from those around it but it was having a domino effect on others and, to his horror, Blake found himself watching the birth of a rock fall.

He yelled his own warning to those on the ground, sent out a silent prayer that the anchor for his own ropes would stay strong and then held his breath as his focus sharpened with such intensity he could feel all the tiny muscles around his eyes contract.

'*Sam*... Get in close...'

She probably couldn't hear his shout because the falling rocks were making their own noise now. A terrifying rumble and crashing.

But she was doing the right thing, not looking up so that her helmet could provide some protection. Flattening herself by clinging to the cliffside so that the rocks were more likely to bounce past. He followed the track of the rocks that were bouncing past her at a reassuring distance, to where those on the ground were running to get themselves clear of danger.

Except for one person.

Harriet was staring up and he could see the horrified expression on her face even from this distance.

Sam was a close friend. She'd been the person who'd put forward the nomination that Sam join this training session.

And now her friend could be in serious trouble. Maybe she felt responsible?

After what felt like the slow motion of watching this begin, it now seemed as if things were on fast forward. The rocks had gone past Sam apparently without injuring her or damaging her ropes but they were gathering momentum as they crashed to ground level.

He could see Jack grab Harriet's arm and pull her away. He saw her start to run.

He saw her trip and fall.

And then he heard someone scream as a rock looked like it landed right on top of her.

A jerk on his rope was enough to reassure Blake that his anchor was still solid. With a sense of urgency unlike anything he could remember experiencing, he let his rope slide and was halfway down the cliff to reach Sam in no more than a few, huge jumps.

He needed to get right down to the bottom to where people were rushing towards Harriet.

But he couldn't go past Sam. She was so still. So frozen. Something had to be wrong and it made him feel sick to his stomach.

This was exactly why he hadn't wanted her on the team in the first place. Because she would be a distraction to whoever got involved with her.

That *he* was that person himself was bad enough.

That he felt the overwhelming urge to protect her above anything else was a wake-up call that hit him as hard as one of those rocks had apparently hit Harriet. Her safety was more important than Harriet's in this instant.

More important than his own.

He *had* to protect her. Had to let her know that she could trust him.

That she could always depend on him.

Dear Lord…he was in *love* with her…

Something he had believed he was safe from ever having to experience.

He didn't get that close to people. *Ever.*

Blake wasn't feeling sick any more.

He felt angry. Angry that Sam had managed to get past his safety walls. Angry that she might be injured.

Just…*angry*…

She couldn't move.

Sam had heard the warning shout from above. She had seen the rocks starting to fall. The terrified whimper that came from her throat was like no sound she had ever heard herself make before.

No…that wasn't true. She *had* made it once before, hadn't she? When she'd been told the terrible news about Alistair.

Killed in a rock fall.

What she was seeing now was quite possibly exactly what her beloved brother had seen in the last few seconds of his life.

She was about to die herself, wasn't she?

Her poor parents…

Terror mixed with the most astonishingly powerful wave of grief. For her parents, for her brother, for herself. It was too big for any kind of release from something as simple as tears. It was crushing her. Making it impossible to breathe. Blurring her vision so that the shape appearing beside her was unrecognisable. Even the voice could barely penetrate the silent scream that was holding her prisoner.

'Sam… *Sam*… Are you listening to me?'

She tried to focus. To hear what Blake was saying.

This was *Blake*… If anyone could keep her safe it would be this man.

'You have to move. The rock fall is over. You're not hurt but we have to get down. *Now*…'

Sam tried to nod her head but that only triggered a shake that instantly spread to the rest of her body. She knew what she needed to do but she couldn't make her hands co-operate. Or her legs.

So she tried to speak but the only sound that emerged was an echo of the distress that had swallowed her the instant she'd seen those rocks begin to fall.

Blake wasn't saying anything now, either. Sam felt his arm slide around her body as he positioned himself behind her. Somehow, he managed to keep her against his body with one arm as he worked both his own ropes and hers with his other arm.

The first drop was difficult and they stopped with a jerk. The second jerky movement finally seemed to break through what had paralysed Sam. Blake was trying to keep her safe but she had to do that for herself, didn't she?

She always had. To protect the people she loved.

Her parents.

Blake...

'You can let me go.' Her voice was rough. 'I can do this now.'

'I don't think so.'

'Let me *go*, Blake.' She pushed his hand away from her ropes and took hold of them herself. 'I can look after myself. I don't need you.'

'Fine.' Blake's arm disappeared as he swung himself to one side.

A minute later they were both at ground level but any relief Sam felt for finishing the abseil without his assistance vanished as her feet hit solid ground and she crumpled because her legs refused to hold her up. She was still shaking. She wanted to apologise to Blake. To try and explain what had happened to make her freeze like that, even, but any words died on her lips as she looked up at him.

Because he looked…angry?

He held her gaze for a long moment. A searching look, as if he was trying to figure out what was wrong with her. And then he gave his head a single, dismissive shake and turned away. The sound of him unclipping his ropes and discarding them was like a punctuation mark. The sound of his boots on rock as he walked swiftly away made it feel completely final.

Sam had never needed human contact more than she did at this moment. She had never felt more alone.

Where was Harriet?

She raked the scene with a wild glance but she couldn't see her best friend anywhere. Nobody was even looking in her direction. They were all clustered to one side, the group opening and then closing again to swallow Blake.

Sam pulled her knees up and then caught them with her arms. It gave her a space to bury her head for a moment. To try and get control of the shaking. To banish what felt like a tsunami of tears that was trying to relentlessly close in on her.

'Harriet?' Blake dropped to his knees beside the limp figure on the ground.

Her face was deathly pale, which made her freckles stand out. Pete was crouched beside her, one hand resting on her shoulder.

'Sorry,' she whispered. 'I'm really sorry, Blake.'

'What on earth for?' Blake had taken hold of her hand but he was using his index finger to feel for her radial pulse.

'I've wrecked our training day…'

The pulse was rapid but steady enough and strong enough to tell him that her blood pressure was not dangerously low.

'Don't be daft…we get to practise some first aid, too, now.'

His gaze was raking his body but he knew that others would have already completed a primary survey. He glanced up. Jack was looking almost as pale as Harriet and he had Luc right beside him.

'Compound fracture,' Luc told him. 'Tib

and fib. She caught a direct hit from a decent-sized rock.'

Luc sounded calm. As though this was nothing that couldn't be dealt with easily. The look he was giving Blake, however, told him that this was more serious and when he dropped his gaze to Harriet's left leg, his heart sank.

It was a mess. An open wound with visible pieces of shattered bone. The risk of infection was huge. The risk of Harriet actually losing her lower leg looked considerable, as well. The potential for irreparable blood supply and nerve damage was obvious.

'Limb baselines?'

'Weak but present.'

Well, that was something. It meant that not all the nerves or blood vessels were damaged beyond repair. 'Is that the only injury?'

Luc nodded. 'Seems to be.'

Jack glared at Blake. 'It's enough, isn't it?'

'It's okay.' Pete seemed to be avoiding looking anywhere near Harriet's leg. 'These guys know what they're doing, babe. It'll be okay, you'll see…'

Someone pushed their way through the silent, horrified group.

'Here's the first-aid kit. And the helicopter's been dispatched. ETA about fifteen minutes.'

Luc was ripping open the zips on the kit. They needed IV gear to get a line in and give Harriet some pain relief. They needed sterile dressings to cover the gaping wound. And they needed a splint. There wasn't much more they could do here. Harriet needed to get to a hospital as fast as possible and into Theatre with the best orthopaedic surgeon that could be found.

They could hear the beat of the approaching helicopter by the time they had Harriet ready for transport. The silent group of onlookers moved back to get out of the way of the paramedics and their stretcher. It took only another minute or two to have Harriet secured but she didn't seem happy. Her head turned from one side to the other and she cried out when the stretcher was lifted.

'No…wait… Where's Sam?'

Blake felt the muscles in his jaw tighten. Sam had not only demonstrated how completely unsuitable she was to join this team, she hadn't even come near her friend who was the one who'd actually been injured in this disaster.

He turned his head to speak to Luc.

'There's no way we're going to let Sam join the SDR,' he said in a low voice. 'She froze up there. Couldn't even follow instructions.'

'*Sam*…' Harriet's call was almost a sob.

'I'm here, Harry…' Sam's quiet voice came from right behind Blake's shoulder.

She moved straight past him. She didn't even glance at him but he knew that she'd heard what he'd said to Luc.

'Oh, God…' Sam was crouching beside the stretcher. 'I'm *so* sorry… I… I messed up.'

'Not as much as I did.' But Harriet was trying to smile. 'Can you come with me, Sam? I'm… I'm really scared…'

'But… I should come with you,' Pete said.

'You hate blood.' Harriet's voice wobbled. 'And hospitals, come to that. I'll see you later…when everything's been fixed, okay?'

'Okay…if that's what you want.' Pete's concerned frown didn't quite disguise his relief.

'Of course I'll come…' But Sam looked towards the paramedics. 'Is there enough room?'

'We can take two extras. No more.'

'I'm coming, too.' Blake ignored Sam, turning to Luc instead. 'Can you take charge now? If people want to carry on with the next climb, that's fine. It'll be a while before we can co-ordinate another day like this but if you decide to wrap things up, that's fine too. Is there anyone who can get my bike back to town?'

'I can.' Jack stepped forward. 'No problem.'

'Don't stop the day,' Harriet said. 'Not on my account. That would make me feel even worse than I do now. Sam...you don't mind missing the rest of it, do you?'

'Of course she doesn't.' Blake couldn't help the acerbic comment. 'She's probably relieved.'

Sam said nothing but he noticed the way her chin lifted a little as she followed Harriet's stretcher to the waiting helicopter.

Any remorse for that less than kind comment, or that she'd overheard him dismissing her bid to join this team, evaporated. She couldn't blame him if she was feeling bad. She hadn't even *tried* to deal with that situation on the cliff face in any meaningful way—just pushed him away when he'd been trying to help. She had ruined any chance of acceptance all by herself.

What seemed worse was that she wasn't the person that Blake had believed her to be.

Where was the courage and determination he'd seen her display on that USAR course? The woman he'd inadvertently fallen in love with?

Maybe something good would come from the catastrophe this day had become.

It would be so much easier to move on now.

CHAPTER NINE

SAM CHOSE TO use the waiting room near Theatre to wait until Harriet's surgery was over.

Blake chose not to. It could be hours and there was no way he was going to sit in a confined space—alone—with Sam.

'Please call me as soon as she's taken through to Recovery,' he told the staff member who'd shown them the room. 'I'll be in the building.'

He didn't look back but he knew that Sam had gone into the empty room with its comfortable chairs and water cooler and supply of magazines.

He knew that she was looking almost as scared as Harriet had looked when they'd finally wheeled her into Theatre. Terrified of the possibility that she could wake up and find she was missing half of her leg.

Blake actually stopped before he got to the elevators.

Turned around, even.

But then he turned back and punched the button to summon the lift.

He had to fight this…

This *pull* to go back to that room. To comfort Sam. To support her. Just to be there with her and hold her hand.

Because, if he didn't fight, he'd be giving in to the last thing he'd ever wanted in his life. To invite somebody into his world who was so important to him they could shape the whole direction of his future.

He'd be throwing away what had always been his dream.

Complete freedom.

He couldn't do that.

He wouldn't allow himself to do that.

Besides…there were things that needed doing. Like finishing the accident report and other paperwork that had been postponed in order to fast track Harriet through Emergency. And he wanted to have a better look at those X-rays.

A comminuted fracture that made it hard to count the number of breaks in her bones.

How on earth were they going to manage to put that back together? That it was already an open wound made it all so much worse. Even with the benefit of IV antibiotics that had already been started, it would take luck to stave off an infection that could destroy more tissue and risk more, debilitating, nerve and blood vessel damage.

He managed to spend over an hour doing that. And then he spent another twenty minutes or more texting Luc to keep him informed about Harriet and to find out what was happening now up in the Blue Mountains. Everybody was worried, apparently, but the consensus of opinion had been that they couldn't waste the resources that had gone into arranging this training session and they were going to see it through.

Still there was no call to tell him that Harriet's surgery was over.

Was Sam still sitting there alone in that room?

Had anyone taken her a coffee? Or something to eat? He didn't like the idea of her being hungry or thirsty.

If he took her something himself, would that mean that he'd lost this internal battle?

No. Blake could feel his frown deepening as he shoved his phone back in his pocket and started walking. It wouldn't actually make any difference if he gave in to this pull because she wasn't about to consider being with him for the rest of her life, was she?

She didn't do relationships. She'd told him that. Or rather she'd agreed with him when he'd said that. When they had been negotiating another 'one-off'. Or a two-off or however many it took before one of them had had enough.

We both walk alone, Blake. For whatever reason...

Why had he never found out what *her* reason was?

It couldn't possibly be as solid as his reason. She hadn't grown up struggling to achieve every step towards a better life or watching someone she loved sacrifice their life for her. She was warm and caring and deserved to be with someone who would reward those attributes by giving them right back to her. And no man in his right mind wouldn't have been attracted from the moment he laid eyes on the most gorgeous woman in the world. She would have had more choice than any woman dreamed of, surely?

So why did she choose to be alone? He didn't understand.

Any more than he understood why she'd lost control so completely on that cliffside. It just didn't make sense. He'd seen her on the climbing wall that night. She knew what she was doing and she had the courage to tackle anything.

He'd seen her at the USAR course and he would have trusted her to face anything and not panic. Blake had been in dodgy situations often enough to learn to trust instincts like this and right now they were telling him that her reaction to that rock fall was completely out of character.

And he had damned her for it.

Guilt was the last straw that tipped the balance in any internal fight that had been ongoing. That, and the idea he'd had that Sam might be hungry.

Was that why his pacing the corridors had somehow brought him so close to the staff cafeteria? There was nothing to stop him getting some takeaway coffees and some food but what would Sam like to eat? There were sandwiches on offer and hot things like sausage rolls and slices of pizza but there were lots of other things like muffins and cookies and he couldn't decide what she would choose if she was standing here herself.

The need to feed Sam had suddenly become the most important thing on his agenda. And he wanted to know what her choice would be so that this wouldn't be so difficult on another occasion. Because there *would* be another occasion in the future. There had to be…

Blake grabbed a handful of paper bags and a pair of tongs to start lifting items from the cabinets.

The worst thing about waiting alone was that there was nowhere to hide from yourself.

No way to distract yourself from thoughts that were dark enough to feed on themselves and become even darker as minutes built into an hour and then started to count down the next.

Nothing to counteract the 'what ifs'.

Like what if she hadn't tried to play down her eagerness to participate and had been one of the first people to go down that cliff? The shock of that rock fall and its effect on her would have been completely private. Something she could have analysed later until she could understand it and excuse herself and then move forward, knowing that she would be able to cope if it ever happened again.

She wouldn't be feeling so disappointed in herself for demonstrating such weakness.

Or so gutted that Blake clearly despised her for it. She could still hear the note of disgust in his voice.

'There's no way we're going to let Sam join the SDR... She froze up there...couldn't even follow instructions...'

And what if Harriet lost her leg? She'd lose everything she loved most about her life. Her job, her work with the SDR team, even the joy she got from surfing and swimming. All the things that made her who she was and the things that she shared with Pete. How would he cope with a disabled partner? Sam had the horrible feeling that he wouldn't cope at all well. He hadn't actually wanted to come with her in the helicopter, had he?

That was incomprehensible. Imagine if it had been Blake who'd been injured? Nothing would have kept her from staying as close as possible. Even if he hadn't wanted her to…

It only needed a split second to change a life, didn't it?

To change many lives, in fact…

How different would her own life have been if Alistair had not died on that mountain? And her parents' lives.

Oddly, the grief that thoughts of her brother always triggered seemed different now. Because she was so worried about Harriet or sad that things with Blake had ended so badly? Or was it that the extraordinary flood of emotion that had been triggered as she'd been caught in the horror of that rock fall had somehow released something that had been buried for what felt like for ever?

Not that Sam could figure out exactly what that might be but there was a sense that it was something peaceful. Like acceptance, perhaps?

Like knowing that random things could happen to anyone no matter how careful they tried to be. That a life could be lost— or changed for ever—in a heartbeat so you had to make the most of every moment and not let others hold you back, no matter how much you loved them.

Blake was going to hold her back now, wasn't he? Could she fight that and ask for another opportunity to prove herself as competent enough to be considered for the team?

Did she *want* to fight the man she loved?

As if her thoughts had somehow conjured him up, Blake appeared in the doorway of this small room. He was balancing a tray of cups in one hand and held a carrier bag stuffed with smaller paper bags in the other.

'I…ah…thought you might be hungry.'

He put the tray of cups down on top of the pile of magazines Sam hadn't thought to leaf through. And then he started unloading the carrier bag onto the low table.

'I wasn't sure what you'd like,' he said.

Such a casual tone, as if it was a normal thing to buy up what looked like half the contents of the cafeteria. Plastic triangles of sandwiches, the tops of muffins and doughnuts to be seen inside paper bags. The smell of something hot and savoury like a sausage roll or those mini mince pies.

He'd thought she might be hungry?

A single sandwich would have been enough.

This felt like it was far more significant than offering food.

It felt like…a peace offering?

She looked up from the feast that had been set out in front of her. Yes…there was something in Blake's eyes that told her she wasn't imagining anything. That this was more than a peace offering, even.

He wanted to give her food because he wanted to show her that he cared.

A lot…

That…that he *loved* her?

A bubble of something Sam couldn't identify grew inside her chest with such intensity it felt like it was going to explode.

And, just at the point of explosion, two things happened.

The pager on Blake's belt sounded. Three buzzes, a short silence and then three more. Sam knew what that meant. A Code One callout for the SDR. Some disaster was changing who knew how many lives out there in this instant of time.

A nurse appeared in the doorway as the pager was sounding for the second time.

'Harriet's in Recovery. She's asking for you guys.'

Blake was on his phone as they walked towards Recovery.

'What is it, Mabel? No, the team's still out in the Blue Mountains as far as I know... Good grief...really...? I know, but I'm here on my own... Try calling Luc and then get back to me asap...'

He cut the call as they neared the IV pumps and other equipment a phone could potentially interfere with. Harriet was drowsy but she managed a smile.

'I've still got my leg,' she murmured.

'That's a great start.' Sam blinked back tears as she stooped to kiss her friend.

Blake was looking at the external fixation on Harriet's leg. 'That's some impressive scaffolding, mate. Does it hurt?'

Harriet shook her head, her eyes drifting shut. 'Morphine's great stuff...'

'I can't stay,' Blake said apologetically. 'There's been a callout and I'm the only one available. Everyone else is still out in the mountains.'

'What's happened?' Sam asked.

'Explosion and fire on a cruise ship that's just out of Sydney harbour. They're sending the coast guard but they need a medical first response. I doubt that any of the other team members will be back in town soon enough to be useful. Sorry...but I have to go.'

Harriet's eyes opened again. Her voice sounded clearer.

'Take Sam with you,' she said.

Blake froze and Sam cringed. Was he going to tell Harriet that he'd dismissed any chance of her being part of this elite team? That she had made a fool of herself by not even being able to follow instructions?

But his gaze caught hers.

'Do you want to come?'

He knew he was taking a risk. But he was prepared to give her another chance?

He wouldn't do that unless he actually believed that she could do it.

Sam could feel her confidence take the biggest leap ever as she sank into that gaze for a heartbeat. And then one more. If Blake believed she could do it then she *could*.

'Yes,' she said quietly. 'I do...'

If someone had been at all inclined to panic, this scenario would have triggered it.

There were steep, narrow metal staircases to climb down into the engine rooms of this huge ship and it was rolling enough to make it difficult. Power was out, so the only illumination was coming from the lamps on their helmets. It was hot and the air was thick with an unpleasant mix of smoke and oil. To top it off, there were strange noises around them with eerie, muted shrieks and banging from metallic structures that were probably cooling down or had been damaged by the explosion and fire.

Sam hadn't missed a beat so far. Blake paused at the bottom of what was hopefully the last tube-like stairwell and watched her come after him. It had been the longest ladder so far and she had to be getting tired but there was no hint of any hesitation. If anything, she was climbing down faster now. She actually jumped to miss the last rung.

'Is this it? Is this where they're trapped?'

The ship's doctor had met them as they'd crouched and run from where the helicopter had landed on the top deck. He'd briefed them as they'd started their journey deeper into the ship.

'One person's been killed and we've got several others with minor injuries and burns.

Most we can manage in our hospital but there's one burns case that needs evacuating.'

'You want us to transport him?'

'If this helicopter can take him back, I've got a nurse who can go with him. There's a bigger problem we need you guys to help with, if you can.'

'What's that?' Blake cast a sideways glance at Sam. She was focused intently on what they were being told. Ready for anything, judging by the serious, determined look on her face.

'There's a couple of people unaccounted for. We think they're trapped somewhere in the engine room behind where the explosion happened. The captain won't let anybody go in there—he says it's too dangerous.'

Blake felt the knot of tension in his gut tighten.

Did he want Sam going in there?

He had no choice now. He had offered her this second chance and this was what the SDR team did. They headed into disasters, not away from them, with the intention of saving lives that might otherwise be lost.

But he was going in first. If it *was* too dangerous, he could change his mind and order Sam to wait on the sidelines.

And now, here they were.

A very challenging environment but it didn't feel too dangerous. Yet.

The man who'd been their guide—one of the ship's fire officers—was still near the bottom of the ladder and he was the one to answer Sam's query.

'We think so. They would have been in that direction. In the next section. We couldn't get near because of the fire but that's all out now and it should be cooling down a bit but...be careful. There's a lot of shredded metal over there.'

Blake nodded. 'Hear that, Sam?'

'Yep.'

'Stay behind me.'

'Okay.'

'Let me know on the radio when you need assistance,' the fire officer said. 'I've got my team ready and stretchers and things available.'

Blake moved forward slowly. The rolling movement of the ship made it even more vital to identify every hazard and the fact that it was Sam who was following him heightened his awareness of anything that could cause harm.

Whenever there was a moment's break or the noise level faded enough, he would pause and call out.

'Rescue team here. Can anyone hear me?'

And ten seconds later, 'Nothing heard.'

'Nothing heard,' Sam would echo.

They squeezed through narrow gaps between enormous metal structures. They climbed over pipes and splashed through deep puddles left behind from the firefighting efforts. The beam of light from Blake's lamp finally raked a warped metal door.

'Rescue team here. Can anyone hear me?'

Another slow roll of the ship happened then and there was a metallic groan as engine parts shifted and scraped. Blake felt Sam touch his arm as she tried to keep her balance. Except she didn't let go.

'I heard something.'

'Background noise.'

'No.' Sam was still holding his arm as she turned her head. 'Rescue team here,' she called loudly. 'Can you hear me?'

This time, Blake could hear the response as well. Faint, but unmistakeable.

'Yes…thank God…' They could hear someone coughing. 'We're in here…'

The door was jammed but the bottom had been bent far enough to create a gap. Not nearly big enough to let Blake get through. Or even one of their backpacks.

'I think I can do it,' Sam said.

'No way. We'll get some more manpower in here. And some cutting gear.'

'That will take too long. What if there's a time-critical injury in there?'

'Hey…' Blake crouched by the bend in the door. 'What's happening in there? Are you hurt?'

'Moz is in a bad way. I think he might be dead. And I'm…bleeding.' The coughing sounded exhausted. 'I can't seem to stop it…'

Sam was pulling her backpack off. 'What's your name?'

'Barry.'

'Try and put some pressure on where you're bleeding, Barry. My name's Sam. I'm going to try and get in to you.'

She knelt on the floor, tilting her head to examine the gap. 'I can't see any sharp edges.'

Looking up, she blinked in the beam of Blake's light. 'Are you sure you want to try this?'

In answer, Sam lay flat on the floor, ignoring the wash of oil-streaked water around her. She lay on her back, her head already in the gap, and then used her feet to push her forward. A few moments later and she had to twist sideways to get her hips through. She felt her overalls snag and rip and could only hope that no skin was involved. Every time she pulled her legs forward she could feel the distance between herself and Blake increase but it didn't matter.

She knew he was there.

And she knew she could do this.

She heard him using the radio to contact the fire officer's team.

'We've found them. We're going to need help.'

Sam scrambled to her knees on the other side of the door. One man lay directly in front of her. Another was slumped in the corner.

'Check Moz first,' the nearest man said. 'Please. He stopped talking to me a while back...'

Barry was gripping his arm. Sam couldn't

see any active bleeding from between his fingers.

She crawled swiftly over to the corner but she knew instantly how unlikely it was that she was going to find a pulse on this man. She could see how bad his head injury was.

She checked anyway.

And then she went straight back to Barry.

'I'm sorry,' she said. 'There's nothing I can do.'

Barry groaned. He let go of his arm and Sam saw a pulse of fresh blood appear. She put her gloved hand over the wound and pressed. Hard.

'I need some dressings, Blake,' she called. 'And bandages.'

He passed them through the gap in the door.

'I'm going to need IV gear as well,' she told him a minute or two later. 'And fluids. Barry? Can you still hear me?'

'What's happening?' Blake's voice was tense. 'Talk to me, Sam.'

'Moz is dead. Head injury.' Sam clipped a tourniquet onto Barry's uninjured arm. 'Barry here has got a deep laceration on his arm but I think I've got the bleeding under control with a pressure bandage. His blood pressure's well down—I can't get a radial pulse and his level of consciousness is dropping.'

'Any other injuries?'

'I don't know. Nothing obvious but I want to get these fluids running and then I'll check more thoroughly.'

'He was coughing. Here's a stethoscope so you can check his lung fields. There could have been a lot of smoke in there.'

'Okay. Give me a second… There… IV's in. I'll just set up the saline and push a bit in.'

She was silent for a minute or two as she worked.

'You okay, Sam?'

'I'm good.'

She could hear the sound of more people arriving behind Blake but the additional sounds didn't quite cover his next words.

'Yeah,' she heard. 'You are…'

CHAPTER TEN

'ARE YOU SURE you don't mind staying behind?'

'No. There's not enough room on the chopper and it's far more important that the rest of the injured people get checked out properly.'

'I'll stay, too, in that case.' Blake's nod was decisive.

'But Barry's your patient.'

'He's stable. And he's in good hands with the paramedics.'

'But the captain says it'll take hours to get towed back into Sydney.'

Blake's eyebrow rose. 'You want me to give up the opportunity for an evening cruise into one of the most beautiful cities in the world? A rare chance to actually relax for a while?'

Sam caught her lip between her teeth. He

wanted to stay on board with her? For hours
and hours?

It almost felt like a date.

'You're not worried about Harriet?'

'I called the hospital. She's sleeping and
probably will until the morning. I left a message to say I'll be in first thing, before I start
work.'

Blake's decision to stay behind meant that
another crew member with minor injuries
could head home to his worried family. As
they watched the rescue helicopter disappear
into the distance, the captain approached to
thank him.

'You both did an amazing job today,' he
said. 'And we want to show you our apprecia-
tion. I'm afraid I'm going to be a bit busy su-
pervising this towing operation but we want
to make one of our staterooms available for
you. You can have a shower and clean up.
We're a bit limited in what we can offer from
our menus, with no power, but we'll do our
best.

A shower...

Sam couldn't stop her lips curving into a
smile.

It was getting even more like a date. Or

rather, like their very first time together, when Blake had offered to let her use the shower in his hotel room. And look how that invitation had turned out…

But maybe he didn't want that to happen again. She risked a quick glance in his direction and something began melting inside her at the brush of pure heat in his eyes.

He was remembering exactly what she was. And he wanted it again as much as she did. Maybe not now. Or here, because that would hardly be appropriate.

But soon…

'Wait here,' the captain instructed. 'Give us a few minutes and then my chief purser will come and get you as soon as we've sorted things.'

It was almost deserted in this area of the top deck where the helipad was located. Sam walked towards the railing to watch the misty outline of the coast becoming clearer. Blake followed her.

'The captain was right,' he said. 'You *did* do an amazing job today.'

Sam smiled. 'Does this mean I'm going to get an invitation to join the team?'

Blake didn't return the smile. 'Do you still want to?'

She caught her breath. She'd been given a second chance to prove herself worthy of the goal that had been so important to her but...was she being given a second chance of something completely different here?

To be on the team—or to be with Blake?

She couldn't tell. But she could sense that the question in his eyes went deeper than whether she still wanted to be a member of the team he was so passionate about.

Sam had to look away. 'You'd really consider that—after what happened today?'

'You mean the way you were totally unfazed by a hostile environment and responded to an emergency without hesitation and pretty much saved a man's life single-handedly?'

'No...' But the praise was doing funny things to her body. Could this glow actually be visible? She didn't dare catch Blake's gaze in case it was. 'I meant what happened on the cliff.'

There was a moment's silence before he spoke quietly. 'What *did* happen, Sam? It wasn't just fear, was it?'

The silence was longer this time but Blake seemed happy to wait.

'A long time ago,' Sam said slowly, 'my older brother, Alistair, got killed in a rock fall.'

'Alistair…' Blake echoed. And then his jaw dropped. 'Alistair Braithwaite was your *brother*?'

'You knew him?'

'I knew *of* him. Who didn't? He was a role model for a lot of young people. He came to speak at my school once and he was inspirational. Bit of a hero of mine, to be honest.'

Sam's smile was poignant. 'Mine, too. I adored him.'

'It was such a tragedy. My God, Sam… I'm not surprised you got overwhelmed. It must have brought everything back in an instant.'

'Too much,' Sam admitted. 'Like how I thought my parents would just disappear into their grief. How it changed our family overnight. We seemed to swap roles somehow. It became my job to protect *them*.'

'I know that feeling. My mum's been pretty dependent on me ever since her stroke.'

'I heard about that.' Sam hesitated for a beat. She was stepping over an unspoken barrier that protected his private life. It took courage to move past it. Almost as much courage as it had taken to start squeezing herself through that narrow gap in the twisted metal door of the engine room. 'It's what stopped you joining MSF, isn't it?'

Blake didn't seem to mind that the barrier had been crossed. 'I love my mum. And I owe her everything but... I'm not proud of it, but I also resented it. I felt like her dependence robbed me of my freedom.'

Sam touched Blake's hand that was gripping the rail in front of her—an automatic gesture of understanding. 'And I felt like Alistair's death robbed me of doing anything exciting ever again. I had to keep myself safe to protect my parents.'

Blake's hand moved to cover hers. 'You didn't keep yourself safe today.'

'I'm not looking forward to telling them about it.' Sam sighed. 'But...but I felt like *me* today. Who I really am. The person I really want to be. And that's important, isn't it?'

She looked up to find Blake smiling at her. The look in his eyes told her that he was about to kiss her but he had something to say first.

'More than important,' he murmured. 'You're not only amazing, Sam Braithwaite. You're very wise.'

The glow that his praise had given her paled into insignificance compared to the one that replaced it as his lips covered hers. It was just the briefest touch but that was okay, because they were in a public place, after all, and were here in a professional capacity.

But life could change in a heartbeat, that was for sure.

And, sometimes, the change was a good one.

Better than anything you might have dreamed of, in fact...

The cabin they were offered was luxurious. Crew T-shirts and track pants had been provided as well, so that they could get out of their oil-streaked, filthy overalls. It was only when Sam was turning to head for the bathroom that Blake noticed the rip in her protective clothing.

'You're not hurt, are you?' It was weird the way his stomach knotted so hard at the thought.

'I don't think so. Only a scratch, if I am.

It's nothing.' Sam's expression was bleak as she looked over her shoulder. 'Do you think Harriet's going to be okay?'

'I think infection's the biggest danger now. Let's hope that doesn't happen.'

'Will she get normal function back again?'

Blake couldn't help his frown. 'It's a nasty injury. That leg is never going to be the same.'

'She'll hate that so much. She loves being on the team so much and every spare minute gets spent outside. It's all the things that she and Pete have in common—surfing, running, the rescue work.'

'Do you think the relationship will survive?'

'I hope so. Harry's got more than enough to deal with already. If you really love someone, going through something like this can make the relationship stronger. What…?' Sam was staring at him. 'Don't you think so?'

'I can't help wondering why he didn't come to the hospital with her.'

'He's not a medic. I think things like that freak him out. And there wasn't enough room in the chopper. Harry asked for me.'

'He didn't jump in his car to follow us, though, did he?'

'No.' Sam was pulling her arms from her overalls. The T-shirt she was wearing underneath rode up and Blake could see the graze on her skin under where the rip had been.

'Let me check that.'

'I'm fine.'

But Blake was already beside her, gently examining the area.

'See? It's just a scratch.'

'It could have been worse.' Blake kept his hand resting on her skin. 'And if it had been, there's no way on earth anyone would have kept me from going to the hospital with you.'

Did she understand what he was trying to tell her?

That he loved her?

The way she reached up to touch his face made it seem like she did understand. And the way she kissed him started to make it seem like she felt exactly the same way.

Until there was a knock at the door and Sam jumped back as though she had been caught doing something unacceptable. Unprofessional, in any case. She disappeared into the bathroom as people started coming into the cabin with trays of food and drink. She was still combing out her hair by the time Blake had taken his turn to shower and change into clean clothes.

'I can't believe this,' she said. 'It's the second time today I've been offered a feast. Oh…' Her eyes widened. 'I've only just realised that we completely forgot about all those things you bought in the cafeteria and it was such a special thing that you did. What a waste.'

'I doubt it was wasted. The nurses would have found it and you know what it's like when there's free food on offer around that place. Besides…' Blake took a step closer to Sam '…even if they didn't find it, it would have been worth it.'

'Why?' This time, it was Sam who stepped closer.

'Because I think you understand why I did it. It said something I couldn't find the words to say.'

Those eyes… The bluest eyes he'd ever seen and right now they were bottomless and he was falling…

'That I need to take care of you,' he added softly. 'To feed you and protect you if, for some reason, it's hard for you to do it for yourself. Because…' He was close enough to touch her now. To pull her into his arms. 'Because you mean so much to me, Sam. I... I love you...'

Those eyes were shining with unshed tears now. 'I love you too, Blake. And I certainly wouldn't be able to find the words to tell you how much.'

He rested his forehead against hers. 'What are we going to do?'

'You mean because neither of us does relationships?'

'Exactly.'

'But we didn't *choose* to make this a relationship. Does that make a difference?'

'I don't know. Maybe.' Blake tightened his hold on Sam. '*Why* don't you do relationships?'

'I've tried. They just don't work so I kind of gave up.'

'Because it's been enough having to protect your parents? That it wouldn't have left enough room for *you* if you'd had someone else to protect as well?'

'Is that why you don't do them?'

'It's more the idea of having someone else dependent on me, I think. Especially children. If something happens, there's no choice but to sacrifice your life for them. Like my mother did for me.'

'I'll bet she didn't see it as a sacrifice. She loves you.'

Blake nodded slowly. 'I know. And now I'm beginning to understand how you could choose to have a bond like that. How it can make even the things that seemed more important than anything else kind of...well, almost irrelevant.'

'We could always go back to what we were doing,' Sam said softly.

'You mean the one-offs until one of us decides that we've had enough? The secret that nobody else knows anything about?'

'Mmm.'

'I don't want it to be a secret any more. I want everyone to know what you mean to me.' Making it public was suddenly important. Because it would make it feel more real? 'I want my mother to get to know you. She's going to love you.'

Sam was grinning. 'My mother's going to be terrified of you. But she'll learn to love you. So will Dad.'

'And I could never have enough,' Blake added. He knew it was true. He didn't want to be without Sam for the rest of his life. For even a day if he could help it.

Sam's smile had faded completely. She had never looked more serious. 'I couldn't either.'

'So…' Blake straightened so that he could see her face properly. 'Maybe we should just bite the bullet and get it over with.'

'Get what over with?'

He could feel one side of his mouth curling upwards. 'The wedding.'

Sam gasped. 'You've got to be kidding me. That could possibly go down in history as the least romantic proposal *ever*.'

Blake slid his hands down Sam's arms to take hold of her hands. He held her gaze as he took a very deep, slow breath.

'I love you,' he said, then. 'More than I ever thought it was possible to love anyone. I thought that sharing my life with someone would somehow stop me being the person I need to be and take away my freedom but…' He caught another breath. 'You *are* my freedom. You said that you felt like you were the person you're meant to be today and that's exactly how I feel when I'm with you. I can't be that person unless you're in my life and I'm asking you to promise me that you'll be there for ever. Will you marry me, Sam?'

Her lips were trembling and those unshed tears that had gathered earlier were now rolling down her face.

'That's *it*... You've found the words I couldn't find. It wasn't just that I was doing exciting, scary stuff today that made me feel like that. It was because I was with *you*. I've felt like that around you ever since...well, maybe ever since you glared at me for dropping that bedpan even though I didn't know it then.' Her words were tumbling out through a misty smile. 'I don't care if it means I can't be on the team. I'd rather be with you. I can't *not* be with you.'

'So...is that a "yes"?'

Sam blinked. 'Didn't I say that already?'

'No.' Blake smiled back at her. 'But I think that's what you meant.'

'Oh...it was. *Is*... Yes, I'll marry you, Blake. I can't think of anything I'd rather do.'

Blake could. Their wedding was too far in the future to think about right now. Not when there was something he'd much rather be doing. Judging by the look in Sam's eyes, she wouldn't be averse to celebrating this engagement in a very personal way. Her next words confirmed that impression.

'Is there a lock on that door?' she whispered.

'I do believe there is.'

'We wouldn't want to get caught, would we…doing something that team members aren't supposed to be doing?'

'We're off duty,' Blake said firmly. 'And I think it's time some of those rules got relaxed a bit, anyway.'

He stepped towards the door and turned the key in the lock.

It didn't feel as if he was keeping something out, however.

It felt like he was letting something in.

A whole new future—for both of them.

It took only another stride to get close enough to Sam to sweep her off her feet and into his arms as he turned towards that deliciously big bed. And now it felt as if he was carrying Sam into that future with him.

And nothing could have felt more right.

* * * * *

Look out for the next story in the
Bondi Bay Heroes quartet

Finding His Wife, Finding a Son
by Marion Lennox

Available now!

And there are two more fabulous
stories to come!

Healed by Her Army Doc
by Meredith Webber

Rescued by Her Mr. Right
by Alison Roberts

Available September 2018!